- 让孩子有一颗纯真的心
- 让孩子有一颗欢乐的心
- 让孩子有一颗向上的心

A Child's Garden of Verses

一个孩子的诗园

〔英〕罗伯特·路易斯·史蒂文森 著

刘荣跃 译

北方联合出版传媒(集团)股份有限公司

万卷出版公司

ⓒ 罗伯特·路易斯·史蒂文森 2021

图书在版编目（CIP）数据

一个孩子的诗园：英、汉／（英）罗伯特·路易斯·
史蒂文森著；刘荣跃译. — 沈阳：万卷出版公司，
2021.3（2024.8重印）
ISBN 978-7-5470-5381-2

Ⅰ.①一… Ⅱ.①罗…②刘… Ⅲ.①儿童诗歌—诗
集—英国—近代—英、汉 Ⅳ.①I561.82

中国版本图书馆CIP数据核字（2020）第103123号

出 品 人：王维良
出版发行：北方联合出版传媒（集团）股份有限公司
　　　　　万卷出版公司
　　　　　（地址：沈阳市和平区十一纬路29号　邮编：110003）
印 刷 者：辽宁新华印务有限公司
经 销 者：全国新华书店
幅面尺寸：145mm×210mm
字　　数：180千字
印　　张：7.75
出版时间：2021年3月第1版
印刷时间：2024年8月第3次印刷
责任编辑：史　丹
责任校对：张兰华
装帧设计：李英辉
ISBN 978-7-5470-5381-2
定　　价：35.00元
联系电话：024-23284090
传　　真：024-23284448

目 录

To Alison Cunningham

第一辑　献给艾莉森·坎宁安

The Child Alone

第二辑　孤独的孩子

Garden Days

第三辑 花园里的日子

Envoys

第四辑　结尾的诗

To Alison Cunningham

From Her Boy

For the long nights you lay awake
And watched for my unworthy sake:
For your most comfortable hand
That led me through the uneven land:
For all the story-books you read:
For all the pains you comforted:

For all you pitied, all you bore,
In sad and happy days of yore: —
My second Mother, my first Wife,
The angel of my infant life—
From the sick child, now well and old,
Take, nurse, the little book you hold!

And grant it, Heaven, that all who read
May find as dear a nurse at need,
And every child who lists my rhyme,
In the bright, fireside, nursery clime,
May hear it in as kind a voice
As made my childish days rejoice!

R. L. S.

献给艾莉森·坎宁安

——她的孩子敬献

·序诗·

为那漫长的黑夜你睡眠消失，
一心照料我这微不足道的孩子；
为您那最让人安慰舒适的巧手，
它带领我在崎岖的路上行走；
为您读过的所有故事书，
为您所缓解的一切痛苦。

为昔日既忧伤又快乐的时候，
一切您所同情所忍耐的忧愁，
我的第二个母亲，第一个妻子，
我婴儿时候的天使——
敬爱的保姆呀，请接受这小小的书本，
它送自一个病孩——如今已是健康的老人。

上帝保佑吧，无论谁读到此书，
都会发现一个危急中献出真情的保姆；
每个孩子阅读这些诗篇——
在明亮的地方，在炉边，在幼儿园——
都会听到一种亲切和蔼的声音，
这声音使我的童年多么欢欣！

罗伯特·路易斯·史蒂文森

一部颇富童趣的少儿诗歌

·译序·

　　本书是英国小说家、散文家和诗人罗伯特·路易斯·史蒂文森（1850—1894）的一部优秀作品，自出版以来深受广大少年儿童的喜爱。它是一部专门为孩子创作的诗歌集，颇富童心童趣，清新活泼，天真纯朴。阅读这样的诗，可以使孩子们有一颗纯真、欢乐和向上的心。孩子从小多读优美的诗歌很有好处，这对他们的健康成长会产生较大的积极影响。我认为青少年时代是读诗的黄金季节，以后参加工作了这样的机会和时间一般来说会相应减少，读诗写诗的人局限在一个较小的范围内——客观现实就是这样的。

本书分为"献给艾莉森·坎宁安""孤独的孩子""花园里的日子"和"结尾的诗"四个部分，约七十首诗歌。第一部分是主体，占了约一半篇幅。诗歌涉及的内容丰富多彩，抒发了书中的"我"作为一名天真活泼的孩子，在童年的各种生活与经历中产生的欢乐、向往和不安等心情。它们不但为儿童所喜爱，就连成人读来也觉得颇富情趣，仿佛自己又回到了从前那天真单纯的难忘岁月，禁不住激动和兴奋——我就是带着这样的心情阅读和翻译本书的。因为喜爱这些诗，所以翻译起来便觉得是一种享受。与孩子们一起回味那美好的时光，不是一件很快乐的事吗？

　　在翻译的过程中我经常为一首首好诗所打动，高兴不已。比如在《夏天的觉》里，作者写他很想再玩一会儿，但必须早早上床睡觉的难过心情，充分体现了儿童的普遍心理。瞧，鸟儿还在树上不停地叫，蓝蓝的天空多么晴朗，街上还传来大人们的脚步声，这个时候又如何能

让满怀好奇的孩子安然入睡呢？孩子们为什么要比大人睡得早呢？诗中的孩子为此感到不安。在《陌生的地方》里，"我"爬上树看见远处陌生而新奇的地方，有花园、河流、人们，对此充满向往。于是"我"希望爬到更高的地方，以便看见更多新奇美好的景象——这不正体现了孩子们强烈的求知欲吗？这个世界是辽阔而神奇的，需要每个人去探索和开发，此诗正刻画出孩子们这种探索的激情。类似的诗颇有一些，如《旅行》《展望》《船向何方？》和《我的床是一只船》等。《我的影子》是一首构思很特别的诗，诗中作者的身影被描绘得惟妙惟肖，简直被写活了。影子时刻跟随着他，与他非常相像，很喜欢变化。可是那天清早它却十分懒惰，在床上睡得又死又沉！这样的诗不胜枚举，读者自可展开想象的翅膀尽情去欣赏，领悟诗中美妙的意趣。

《一个孩子的诗园》中的这些诗，语言十分朴实，清新活泼，读来像一阵清风拂面，令人畅快。我喜欢这种朴实的短诗，我认为好诗不在于语言的华丽，而在于其中所体现的意境。我之所以特别喜欢著名诗人艾青的诗，就是这个原因。我觉得艾青的诗非常朴实，但却很能打动人心，令人回味无穷。二十多年前读到的《大堰河——我的保姆》和《鱼化石》等诗歌，令我深受触动，终生难忘。它们的语言看似简单，却包含着浓浓的诗意，非普通的诗所能企及。我认为本诗集也是用平凡的语言写出了不平凡的诗情，值得玩味。

诗除了要有好的意境外，韵律也是一个很重要的方面，特别是儿童诗。诗是用来朗读的，诗能朗朗上口本身就给人一种美感，所以诗应该是要押韵的。本书译文特别注重这一点，在韵律上力求与原诗同步。中国诗与英美诗的韵律各有特点，中国诗一般是一韵到底或每节一韵，韵律变化相对较少；英美诗的韵律则变化较多，如每两行一韵、每隔一行一韵等，可用字母表示为"aabb ccdd""abab cdcd"。为了让读者对此有更多的体会，本书特对每首诗的韵律给予注明——我认为这是有必要的，也算是这部译本的一个特点吧。根据我的经验，不少中国读者对外国诗的韵律不一定很清楚，或至少认识不够充分。多年前我读外国诗就是这样的，后来读到名家的介绍，才真正懂得了外国诗的韵律特点。我们学习外国诗，应该知道它们是如何押韵的。

另外，本书中的原文有的词看似有误，实则本身如此，是古英语用法，阅读时应予注意。如'shamed 即 ashamed, o'erhead 即 overhead, ev'ry 即 every, maketh 即 makes, o'er 即 over。

　　罗伯特·路易斯·史蒂文森是一位多产的作家，小说、散文和诗歌均有创作。他出生于爱尔兰的一个工程师家庭，1868 年进入爱丁堡大学学习土木工程，后来改学法律，最终弃法从文。他爱好冒险，搜奇猎异，

所以他的作品内容大多是新奇浪漫的冒险故事，他也因此有了冒险小说家的美誉。他的小说故事引人入胜，文笔优美简洁，流传很广。其作品有：《金银岛》《化身博士》《黑箭》《绑架》和《新天方夜谭》等。《金银岛》是他创作的第一部长篇小说，也是他的代表作之一，写的是18世纪时青年吉姆到某座岛上去寻宝的冒险故事。这部作品情节奇异，场面动人，开创了以发掘宝藏为小说题材的先河，问世后轰动一时。《化身博士》也是比较著名的一部小说，描写人身上善与恶的斗争。除小说和散文外，史蒂文森还创作有不少诗歌，作品有：《民歌民谣》《一个孩子的诗园》《旅行之歌》和《新诗》等。他把不平凡的事物和日常实际生活相对照，重视人的勇敢、毅力、正直与诚实的品德，作品风格优美，文笔细腻流畅，富于想象力。

我很高兴成为本书的译者，因为我很喜欢优秀的诗歌，也因为我曾为诗"疯狂"过一阵——那是三十多年前的事了。记得当时年轻的我读了不少诗，也写了不少"诗"，那种激情我至今仍然记忆犹新。灵感不断涌现，一涌现就抓起什么纸片赶紧记下来，竟然也写了厚厚一大沓！我曾梦想着成为一名诗人——那时的梦想何止是诗人！但多年后的今天我并没有成为诗人，而是成了一名已出版二十七部译著约五百万字的译者。不过想来那段为诗而"疯狂"的日子并非没有意义。从事文学翻译必须要有文学激情和冲动，否则翻译出来的东西便会枯燥乏味。我没有成为诗人，但成了诗歌的译者，这也算是满足了我那份喜爱诗歌的情结吧！于是我也获得了同样的喜悦。

这本经典童诗的译著曾于 2002 年由重庆出版社出版。此次重新出版，笔者又认真进行了修订，对部分地方的韵律和含义做了一定的调整。相信这个版本比前一个拙译更加完善。但追求完善的路是没有止境的。书中的错误和遗漏在所难免，诚恳希望广大读者、同人和专家不吝指教，以便不断修正。

刘荣跃

A CHILD'S GARDEN of Verses

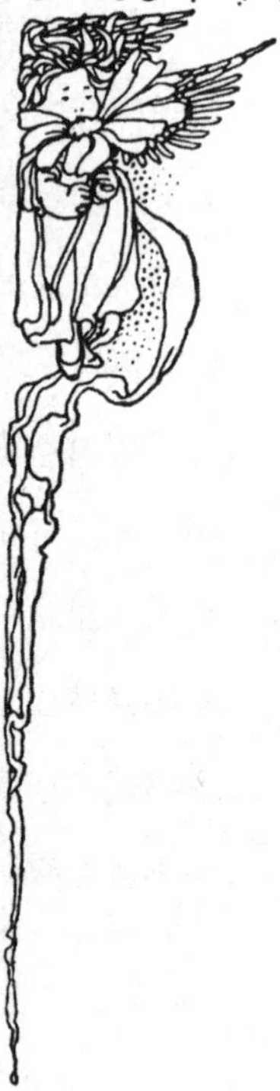

To Alison
Cunningham

第 一 辑

献给艾莉森·坎宁安

Bed in Summer

In winter I get up at night
And dress by yellow candle-light.
In summer, quite the other way,
I have to go to bed by day.

I have to go to bed and see
The birds still hopping on the tree,
Or hear the grown-up people's feet
Still going past me in the street.

And does it not seem hard to you,
When all the sky is clear and blue,
And I should like so much to play,
To have to go to bed by day?

夏天的觉

冬天里我天没亮就起床，
穿衣服需要暖黄的烛光。
但是夏天里却完全不同了，
天没黑我就必须去睡觉。

我必须早早上床躺着，
可鸟儿还在树上不停地跳哟；
我听见大人们的脚步声音，
仍在街上响个不停。

难道你不觉得十分难过吗？
看蓝蓝的天空多么晴朗呀，
我真想出去玩得开心舒畅，
可天还亮着就必须躺到床上。①

---

① 本诗韵律为aabb ccdd eeff。

A Thought

It is very nice to think

The world is full of meat and drink,

With little children saying grace

In every Christian kind of place.

一个想法

想到世上有很多肉食和饮料，
我的心里便感到多么美妙；
在每个信仰基督教的地点，
小孩子们把祈祷放在最前。①

①本诗韵律为aabb。

At the Sea-Side

When I was down beside the sea
A wooden spade they gave to me
To dig the sandy shore.

My holes were empty like a cup.
In every hole the sea came up,
Till it could come no more.

在海边

当我漫步在海边,
他们给我一把木铲,
我用它在沙滩上挖坑。

坑挖得像一只只空杯,
蓝蓝的海水涌入坑内,
直到把坑装得满满登登。 ①

---

① 本诗韵律为aab ccb。

Young Night-Thought

All night long and every night,
When my mama puts out the light,
I see the people marching by,
As plain as day before my eye.

Armies and emperor and kings,
All carrying different kinds of things,
And marching in so grand a way,
You never saw the like by day.

So fine a show was never seen
At the great circus on the green;
For every kind of beast and man
Is marching in that caravan.

As first they move a little slow,
But still the faster on they go,
And still beside them close I keep
Until we reach the town of Sleep.

小孩的夜思

在每个漫长的夜晚，
当妈妈把灯一关，
我就看见走过一支队伍，
正如白天一样清楚。

有军队、国王和皇帝，
人人拿着不同的东西，
他们行进得如此雄壮，
白天可看不到这番景象。

即便草地上的大型马戏团，
也从未演出过这样的奇观；
因为在这支庞大的队伍里，
各种兽与人行进在一起。

他们最初走得较慢，
后来速度加快，持续不断，
我紧紧地跟随着他们，
直至到达睡眠之城。①

---

① 本诗韵律为aabb ccdd eeff gghh。

Whole Duty of Children

child should always say what's true

And speak when he is spoken to,

And behave mannerly at table;

At least as far as he is able.

孩子的全部责任

孩子总应该讲真话，
别人对他说话时要有应答，
餐桌上要有礼貌；
至少应该尽量做到。[1]

---

① 本诗韵律为aabb。

Rain

The rain is raining all around,

It falls on field and tree,

It rains on the umbrellas here,

And on the ships at sea.

雨

雨到处下着，

落到地里和树上，

落到这一把把雨伞上面，

还落到了大海中的船上。①

---

① 本诗为无韵诗。

Pirate Story

Three of us afloat in the meadow by the swing,

Three of us aboard in the basket on the lea.

Winds are in the air, they are blowing in the spring,

And waves are on the meadow like the waves there are at sea.

Where shall we adventure, to-day that we're afloat,

Wary of the weather and steering by a star?

Shall it be to Africa, a-steering of the boat,

To Providence, or Babylon or off to Malabar?

Hi! but here's a squadron a-rowing on the sea—

Cattle on the meadow a-charging with a roar!

Quick, and we'll escape them, they're as mad as they can be,

The wicket is the harbour and the garden is the shore.

海盗的故事

我们三人打着秋千在牧场上飘浮，
我们三人坐在篮中荡漾于草地之上。
春天的风儿在空中轻轻吹拂，
草地的波浪与大海的一模一样。

今天我们将冒险飘向何地？
我们警惕着天气，在星星的指引下远航——
它将把船儿引向非洲那里，
还是去往普罗维登斯、马拉巴尔或巴比伦①的方向？

嗨！这儿是一支行驶于海上的中队，
牛群怒号着在草地上奔驰如飞一般！
咱们得赶紧摆脱疯狂无比的它们，无论是谁，
那小门是港口，花园是海岸。②

---

① 普罗维登斯，美国罗得岛州首府。马拉巴尔，印度西南部一沿海地区。
巴比伦，古代东方一奴隶制国家。
② 本诗韵律为abab cdcd efef。

8

Foreign Lands

Up into the cherry tree
Who should climb but little me?
I held the trunk with both my hands
And looked abroad in foreign lands.

I saw the next door garden lie,
Adorned with flowers, before my eye,
And many pleasant places more
That I had never seen before.

I saw the dimpling river pass
And be the sky's blue looking-glass;
The dusty roads go up and down
With people tramping in to town.

If I could find a higher tree
Farther and farther I should see,
To where the grown-up river slips
Into the sea among the ships,

To where the road on either hand
Lead onward into fairy land,
Where all the children dine at five,
And all the playthings come alive.

陌生的地方

除了小小的我之外，
谁会爬到这樱桃树上来？
我用双手把树干抱住，
看陌生的地方，在远处。

我看见隔壁有一座花园，
美丽的鲜花就在眼前。
我还看见许多可爱的地点，
它们都是我第一次所见。

我看见河水涟漪不断，
它是天空蓝色的镜面；
只见路上尘土不断飞扬，
许多人赶着要去镇上。

我如果爬到一棵更高的大树之上，
就能看到更远更远的地方。
那儿有一条大河在涌动，
它悄然流入船只往来的海中。

我还看到两边的大路，
通向前面的仙境之都，
那里所有孩子五点钟吃饭，
他们的玩具都好像活了一般。①

———————
① 本诗韵律为aabb ccdd eeff gghh iijj。

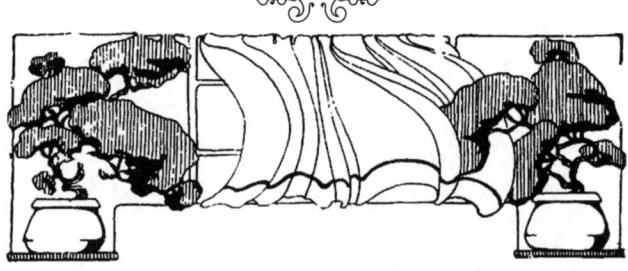

Windy Nights

Whenever the moon and stars are set,

Whenever the wind is high,

All night long in the dark and wet,

A man goes riding by.

Late in the night when the fires are out,

Why does he gallop and gallop about?

Whenever the trees are crying aloud,

And ships are tossed at sea,

By, on the highway, low and loud,

By at the gallop goes he.

By at the gallop he goes, and then

By he comes back at the gallop again.

刮风的夜晚

无论何时月亮和星星隐去，
无论何时刮起大风，
在黑暗的长夜，下着雨，
一个男人总会骑马向前猛冲。
夜深了，炉火已毫无剩余，
他为何还骑着马，从心所欲？

无论何时树林发出狂叫，
船儿在海上颠簸不停，
他骑着马闪过，声音时大时小，
那是他在公路上穿行。
他骑马飞奔而过，一分钟不到
又骑着马踏上回归之道。①

---

① 本诗韵律为ababcc dedeff。

Travel

I should like to rise and go

Where the golden apples grow; —

Where below another sky

Parrot islands anchored lie,

And, watched by cockatoos and goats,

Lonely Crusoes building boats; —

Where in sunshine reaching out

Eastern cities, miles about,

Are with mosque and minaret

Among sandy gardens set,

And the rich goods from near and far

Hang for sale in the bazaar; —

Where the Great Wall round China goes,

And on one side the desert blows,

And with bell and voice and drum,

Cities on the other hum; —

Where are forests, hot as fire,

Wide as England, tall as a spire,

Full of apes and cocoa-nuts

And the negro hunters' huts; —

Where the knotty crocodile

Lies and blinks in the Nile,

And the red flamingo flies

Hunting fish before his eyes; —

Where in jungles, near and far,

Man-devouring tigers are,

Lying close and giving ear

Lest the hunt be drawing near,

Or a comer-by be seen

Swinging in the palanquin; —

Where among the desert sands

Some deserted city stands,

All its children, sweep and prince,

Grown to manhood ages since,

Not a foot in street or house,

Not a stir of child or mouse,

And when kindly falls the night,

In all the town no spark of light.

There I'll come when I'm a man

With a camel caravan;

Light a fire in the gloom

Of some dusty dining-room;

See the pictures on the walls,

Heroes, fights and festivals;

And in a corner find the toys

Of the old Egyptian boys.

旅行

我喜欢早早起床，
去有金苹果的地方；
那儿是另一片蓝天，
鹦鹉岛在此固守江山；
孤独的鲁滨孙们造着船，
小鹦鹉和山羊在旁边陪伴。
那儿阳光普照大地，
一座座东方城市占据辽阔面积，
清真寺和尖塔位于市里，
它们各自在沙地花园中矗立；
来自远近的丰富商品在等候，
它们悬挂于集市内供出售；

那儿长城把中国环绕，
一边的荒沙在猛跑；
座座城市位于另一边，
人声和钟鼓声回荡在耳畔；
那儿有热得似火的森林，
像塔顶般高耸入云，像英国般广阔无垠；
猿猴和椰子不少，
黑人猎手的棚屋四处能见到；
那儿满身突起的鳄鱼出现，
趴在尼罗河上眨着两眼；
红红的火烈鸟一下飞过，
在它眼前把鱼追捉；
那儿附近和远处的丛林，
有老虎时而会吃人；
它们趴在周围倾听，
以便防止猎人靠近；
或出现一个新来者，
他坐在轿里摇晃，是个旅客；
那儿在一片沙地之上，
某座城市已经荒凉；
所有孩子无论地位高下，
后来都一个个长大；
街上和房里没一个脚印，
也不见任何孩子和老鼠穿行；
当夜幕温和地到来，

全城没有一丝光彩。
我长大后打算去那里，
让一支骆驼队伍和我一起；
在某间餐室中——它灰尘已积满——
点燃炉火驱散黑暗；
我观看墙上的绘画一幅幅，
战斗英雄和喜庆佳节显现于各处；
我在屋角发现一些玩具，
它们都是男孩，从古埃及获取。 ①

---

① 本诗整体韵律为aa bb cc dd ee……，有少量重复韵脚。

11

Singing

Of speckled eggs the birdie sings
And nests among the trees;
The sailor sings of ropes and things
In ships upon the seas.

The children sing in far Japan,
The children sing in Spain;
The organ with the organ man
Is singing in the rain.

歌唱

为带斑点的蛋歌唱，
在树林中筑起了窝；
水手在海里的船上歌唱，
唱各种东西也包括缆索。

在遥远的西班牙和日本，
也有孩子在唱歌；
甚至风琴和演奏它的人，
也在雨中唱起了歌。①

————

① 本诗韵律为abab cdcd。

Looking Forward

When I am grown to man's estate

I shall be very proud and great,

And tell the other girls and boys

Not to meddle with my toys.

展望

当我长成大人的时候，
我将非常自豪和优秀；
我要告诉其他孩子，无论男女，
请别乱动我的玩具。①

---

① 本诗韵律为aabb。

A Good Play

We built a ship upon the stairs
All made of the back-bedroom chairs,
And filled it full of soft pillows
To go a-sailing on the billows.

We took a saw and several nails,
And water in the nursery pails;
And Tom said, "Let us also take
An apple and a slice of cake; "—
Which was enough for Tom and me
To go a-sailing on, till tea.

We sailed along for days and days,
And had the very best of plays;
But Tom fell out and hurt his knee,
So there was no one left but me.

一个好游戏

我们在楼梯上造出一只小船——
全部用后卧室的椅子把它做完，
船里填满柔软的大枕，
我们就此在巨浪上开始航程。

我们带了几颗钉子和一把锯，
又将水往幼儿园的小桶添去；
汤姆说："咱们另外还要
一个苹果和一块蛋糕。"
两人吃已经足够，
可以航行到吃茶点的时候。

我们一天又一天驶向远方，
玩着最美好的游戏多么欢畅；
可是汤姆掉出船外弄伤两膝，
剩下我一人待在船里。①

———————

① 本诗韵律为aabb ccddee ffgg。

14

Where Go the Boats?

Dark brown is the river,
Golden is the sand.
It flows along for ever,
With trees on either hand.

Green leaves a-floating,
Castles of the foam,
Boats of mine a-boating—
Where will all come home?

On goes the river

And out past the mill,

Away down the valley,

Away down the hill.

Away down the river,

A hundred miles or more,

Other little children

Shall bring my boats ashore.

船向何方？

黑褐色的河流，
金黄色的沙滩。
河水永不停留，
两岸树林成片。

绿叶漂浮在水面，
一座座泡沫城堡向前行驶，
它们是我的一只只小船——
将要漂向哪里才能停止？

河水永不停步，
流过面粉厂家，
流过溪谷，
又流过山丘之下。

河水不断向下漂流，
流了一百多英里那么遥远，
别处的小孩看见的时候
会把我的船儿弄上岸边。①

---

① 本诗韵律为abab cdcd efef ghgh。

Auntie's Skirts

Whenever Auntie moves around,

Her dresses make a curious sound,

They trail behind her up the floor,

And trundle after through the door.

阿姨的裙子

每当阿姨在屋里走个不停，
裙子就发出奇特的声音，
移过地板时拖在她身后，
然后转动着穿出门口。①

---

① 本诗韵律为aabb。

The Land of Counterpane

When I was sick and lay a-bed,

I had two pillows at my head,

And all my toys beside me lay

To keep me happy all the day.

And sometimes for an hour or so

I watched my leaden soldiers go,

With different uniforms and drills,

Among the bed-clothes, through the hills;

And sometimes sent my ships in fleets

All up and down among the sheets;

Or brought my trees and houses out,

And planted cities all about.

I was the giant great and still

That sits upon the pillow-hill,

And sees before him, dale and plain,

The pleasant land of counterpane.

床上大陆

当我生病躺卧在床，
我把头搁在两个枕上，
所有玩具放在身边，
整天我都觉得心欢。

有时我花去大约一小时，
观看铅制士兵行进不止，
它们穿过床单被褥组成的山丘，
各种制服与操练应有尽有。

有时我派出一支支舰队，
让它们颠簸起伏在床单内，
或者我搬出树林和房屋，
把城市修建在各处。

我是巨人，庞大而平静，
巍然矗立在枕头山顶，
面对眼前的平原和溪谷——
让人多么快乐的床上大陆。[1]

---

[1] 本诗韵律为aabb ccdd eeff gghh。

17

The Land of Nod

From breakfast on through all the day
At home among my friends I stay,
But every night I go abroad
Afar into the land of Nod.

All by myself I have to go,
With none to tell me what to do—
All alone beside the streams
And up the mountain-sides of dreams.

The strangest things are these for me,
Both things to eat and things to see,
And many frightening sights abroad
Till morning in the land of Nod.

Try as I like to find the way,
I never can get back by day,
Nor can remember plain and clear
The curious music that I hear.

睡梦之乡

我从早餐直到晚饭，
在家里陪朋友们一整天，
每夜我都要去外面游荡，
踏上远方的睡梦之乡。

我不得不独自出行
没人告诉我做什么事情——
我一个人经过溪水旁
爬向梦中的山腰之上。

这儿我得到的东西最为奇怪，
吃的和看的无处不在，
又有许多让人惊恐的场面，
个个消失在早晨之前。

我想努力找到回家的路线，
但是白天它们都不曾出现，
即使我听见过奇怪的音乐，
也无法清清楚楚地记得。①

---

① 本诗韵律为aabb ccdd eeff gghh。

18

My Shadow

I have a little shadow that goes in and out with me,

And what can be the use of him is more than I can see.

He is very, very like me from the heels up to the head;

And I see him jump before me, when I jump into my bed.

The funniest thing about him is the way he likes to grow—

Not at all like proper children, which is always very slow;

For he sometimes shoots up taller like an india-rubber ball,

And he sometimes goes so little that there's none of him at all.

He hasn't got a notion of how children ought to play,

And can only make a fool of me in every sort of way.

He stays so close beside me, he's a coward you can see;

I'd think shame to stick to nursie as that shadow sticks to me!

One morning, very early, before the sun was up,

I rose and found the shining dew on every buttercup;

But my lazy little shadow, like an arrant sleepy-head,

Had stayed at home behind me and was fast asleep in bed.

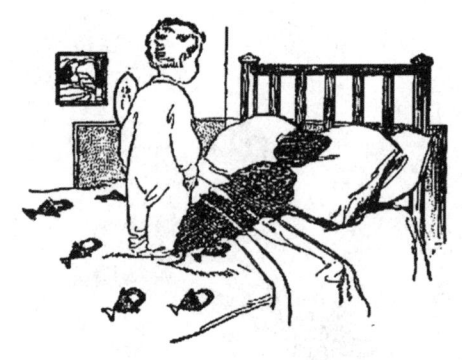

我的影子

我有一个小影与我一起进出，
它有什么用处我一点不清楚。
它从头到脚非常非常像我，
我跳上床时看见它已跳上去啰。

它最有趣的是特别喜欢变化——
一点不像规矩的孩子慢慢长大；
它有时像个皮球弹得比我还高，
有时又缩小得几乎无法看到。

它完全不知道孩子们应怎样玩耍，
只会想尽办法把我捉弄一下。
它紧紧跟在我身边，你看出它真是没胆，
我觉得老跟着保姆（像它老跟着我）实在丢脸。

一天清早当太阳还没升起，
我起床发现所有毛茛上露珠熠熠；
可是我懒惰的小影像个最最贪睡的人，
待在床上睡得又死又沉。①

---

① 本诗韵律为aabb ccdd eeff gghh。

19

System

Every night my prayers I say,

And get my dinner every day;

And every day that I've been good,

I get an orange after food.

The child that is not clean and neat,

With lots of toys and things to eat,

He is a naughty child, I'm sure—

Or else his dear papa is poor.

规律

我每晚都要做祈祷，
每天的饮食必不可少；
我每天的生活过得不错，
饭后总要吃橘子一个。

那个孩子对整洁并不注意，
他有很多玩具和吃的东西；
他是个淘气的孩子，我肯定——
不然他亲爱的爸爸就很清贫。①

---

① 本诗韵律为aabb ccdd。

20

A Good Boy

I woke before the morning, I was happy all the day,
I never said an ugly word, but smiled and stuck to play.

And now at last the sun is going down behind the wood,
And I am very happy, for I know that I've been good.

My bed is waiting cool and fresh, with linen smooth and fair,
And I must be off to sleepsin-by, and not forget my prayer.

I know that, till to-morrow I shall see the sun arise,
No ugly dream shall fright my mind, no ugly sight my eyes.

But slumber hold me tightly till I waken in the dawn,
And hear the thrushes singing in the lilacs round the lawn.

一个好男孩

我在早晨醒来，整天感到心欢，
我从不说脏话，微笑着只顾游玩。

现在太阳终于要从树林后沉落，
我多么高兴，知道自己一直不错。

整洁凉快的床等着我，亚麻床单好得不得了，
我得回去睡觉啦，可不能忘了祈祷。

我知道要明天才能看见太阳升起，
不会有噩梦来骚扰我，眼前也不会出现吓人的东西。

可我陷入沉沉的梦乡，醒来时天已大亮，
只听见画眉在草坪周围的丁香里放声歌唱。①

---

① 本诗韵律为aa bb cc dd ee。

21

Escape at Bedtime

The lights from the parlour and kitchen shone out

Through the blinds and the windows and bars;

And high overhead and all moving about,

There were thousands of millions of stars.

There ne'er were such thousands of leaves on a tree,

Nor of people in church or the Park,

As the crowds of the stars that looked down upon me,

And that glittered and winked in the dark.

The Dog, and the Plough, and the Hunter, and all,

And the star of the sailor, and Mars,

These shone in the sky, and the pail by the wall

Would be half full of water and stars.

They saw me at last, and they chased me with cries,

And they soon had me packed into bed;

But the glory kept shining and bright in my eyes,

And the stars going round in my head.

不想睡觉

灯光照射出客厅和厨房，
穿过窗帘、窗口和窗栏；
数百万星星高高在上，
颗颗都在移动不断。
树上的叶子都没星星那么多，
教堂和公园里的人群也不能与之相比；
无数星星呀正俯瞰着我，
它们一闪一闪地眨眼在黑夜里。

天狼，北斗，猎户，不管什么种类，
还有水手之星与火星，
无不闪烁在天空，而墙边的桶内，
也一半是水一半是星星。
它们终于看见我，叫着把我追踪，
不久将我赶到床上去了；
但那光辉仍鲜明地呈现在我眼中，
每颗星星都旋转于我头脑。①

---

① 本诗韵律为ababcdcd efefghgh。

22

Marching Song

Bring the comb and play upon it!

Marching, here we come!

Willie cocks his highland bonnet,

Johnnie beats the drum.

Mary Jane commands the party,

Peter leads the rear;

Feet in time, alert and hearty,

Each a Grenadier!

All in the most martial manner

Marching double-quick;

While the napkin, like a banner,

Waves upon the stick!

Here's enough of fame and pillage,

Great commander Jane!

Now that we've been round the village,

Let's go home again.

行军曲

拿起梳子，吹响号角！
前进，我们来到！
威利翘起他的苏格兰童帽，
约翰尼把鼓猛敲。

马利·琼指挥队伍向前挺进，
彼得紧紧跟在后面；
每人都是一个精兵，
脚步合着节拍，机警而强健！

全体队员燃起斗志，
这时整齐地向前快跑；
餐巾就像一面旗帜，
在一支棍上面猛飘！

这儿的荣誉和战利品很多，
琼司令是多么伟大！
现在我们已把村庄绕过，
请各自分别回家。 ①

---

① 本诗韵律为abab cdcd efef ghgh，中文译诗部分韵脚有重复。

23

The Cow

The friendly cow all red and white,

I love with all my heart:

She gives me cream with all her might,

To eat with apple-tart.

She wanders lowing here and there,

And yet she cannot stray,

All in the pleasant open air,

The pleasant light of day;

And blown by all the winds that pass

And wet with all the showers,

She walks among the meadow grass

And eats the meadow flowers.

母牛

一身红白花纹的母牛是我好友，
我全心全意地爱着她。
她尽一切努力给我奶油，
让我涂在苹果馅饼上吃下。

她低着头四处漫步，
却从不会迷失方向；
室外的空气多么舒服，
还有和煦温暖的阳光。

路过的风无不吹到她身体，
阵雨把她浑身都打湿了；
她漫步在草地里，
吃着其中的花草。①

---

① 本诗韵律为abab cdcd efef。

Happy Thought

The world is so full of a number of things,

I'm sure we should all be as happy as kings.

欢乐思想

世界上的事物有
许许多多，
我深信大家都
应像国王一样
欢乐哟。①

---

① 本诗韵律为aa。

The Wind

I saw you toss the kites on high
And blow the birds about the sky;
And all around I heard you pass,
Like ladies' skirts across the grass—
O wind, a-blowing all day long,
O wind, that sings so loud a song!

I saw the different things you did,
But always you yourself you hid.
I felt you push, I heard you call,
I could not see yourself at all—
O wind, a-blowing all day long,
O wind, that sings so loud a song!

O you that are so strong and cold,

O blower, are you young or old?

Are you a beast of field and tree,

Or just a stronger child than me?

O wind, a-blowing all day long,

O wind, that sings so loud a song!

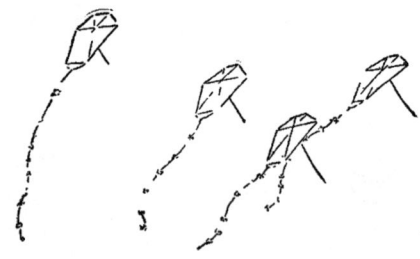

风

我看见你把风筝抛向高空，
吹得鸟儿在天上转动；
我听见你从四处经过，
像女士的裙子在草地上拖着——
啊风儿，你整天不停地吹响，
啊风儿，你的歌声多么嘹亮！

我看过你做的各种事情，
但你总是把自己藏隐。
我感到你的推动，听见你的呼叫，
却无法把你寻找——
啊风儿，你整天不停地吹响，
啊风儿，你的歌声多么嘹亮！

啊，你既强大又严寒，
啊风儿，你是青年还是老年？
你是旷野和树中的野兽，
或者只是你的威力我没有？
啊风儿，你整天不停地吹响，
啊风儿，你的歌声多么嘹亮！①

———————

① 本诗韵律为aabbcc ddeecc ffggcc。

26

Keepsake Mill

Over the borders, a sin without pardon,
Breaking the branches and crawling below,
Out through the breach in the wall of the garden,
Down by the banks of the river we go.

Here is a mill with the humming of thunder,
Here is the weir with the wonder of foam,
Here is the sluice with the race running under—
Marvellous places, though handy to home!

Sounds of the village grow stiller and stiller,
Stiller the note of the birds on the hill;
Dusty and dim are the eyes of the miller,
Deaf are his ears with the moil of the mill.

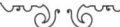

Years may go by, and the wheel in the river
Wheel as it wheels for us, children, to-day,
Wheel and keep roaring and foaming for ever
Long after all of the boys are away.

Home for the Indies and home from the ocean,
Heroes and soldiers we all shall come home;
Still we shall find the old mill wheel in motion,
Turning and churning that river to foam.

You with the bean that I gave when we quarrelled,
I with your marble of Saturday last,
Honoured and old and all gaily apparelled,
Here we shall meet and remember the past.

磨坊纪念物

翻过边沿，我们犯下不可饶恕的错误：
折断树枝，从下面爬出来，
又从庭园的墙缝中穿出，
然后沿着河岸离开。

这儿有一座磨坊发出嗡嗡之声，
这儿有泛着奇特泡沫的水坝，
这儿有急流从水闸下飞奔——
多么神奇的地方，虽然不远就是我家！

村子里越来越平静，
山上鸟儿的歌声越来越稀少；
磨坊主眨着模糊的眼睛，
他耳朵失灵是因辛苦地操劳。

河中的水轮或许很多年后，
仍将为我们这些孩子旋转，
泛出白沫，永不停息地叫吼，
直至所有男孩早已走完。

后来我们去了印度群岛，又凯旋自大海之中，
个个成为英雄和士兵；
我们发现陈旧的水轮还在转动，
河水搅出的泡沫仍然白得似银。

你带着我们吵架时我给你的豆子，
我带着你最后那个星期六给我的弹球，
我们都已年老而光荣，身穿鲜艳服饰，
相聚在这里回忆往昔时候。①

---

① 本诗韵律为abab cdcd efef ghgh ijij klkl。

27

Good and Bad Children

Children, you are very little,
And your bones are very brittle;
If you would grow great and stately,
You must try to walk sedately.

You must still be bright and quiet,
And content with simple diet;
And remain, through all bewild'ring,
Innocent and honest children.

Happy hearts and happy faces,
Happy play in grassy places—
That was how, in ancient ages,
Children grew to kings and sages.

But the unkind and the unruly,
And the sort who eat unduly,
They must never hope for glory—
Theirs is quite a different story!

Cruel children, crying babies,
All grow up as geese and gabies,
Hated, as their age increases,
By their nephews and their nieces.

好孩子与坏孩子

孩子呀，你们多么小哟，
你们的骨头真是脆弱；
如果要健康茁壮成长，
就必须走路端庄。

你还必须朴实而伶俐，
粗茶淡饭从不厌弃；
置身让人迷惑的世界中，
始终做个纯真诚实的孩童。

心情快乐喜形于色，
在绿草地上玩得多么喜悦——
古时的孩子就是这样，
最后成为圣人和皇上。

但有的孩子不守规矩不懂仁慈，
有的又只知大喝大吃，
他们永远别想获得光荣——
他们的生活真是迥然不同！

让人痛苦的孩子，哭叫的婴孩，
长大后无不成为傻瓜和蠢材，
随着他们年龄的递增，
侄儿侄女都会把他们怨恨。①

---

① 本诗韵律为aabb ccdd eeff gghh iijj。

28

Foreign Children

Little Indian, Sioux, or Crow,

Little frosty Eskimo,

Little Turk or Japanee,

Oh! don't you wish that you were me?

You have seen the scarlet trees

And the lions over seas;

You have eaten ostrich eggs,

And turned the turtles off their legs.

Such a life is very fine,

But it's not so nice as mine:

You must often as you trod,

Have wearied NOT to be abroad.

You have curious things to eat,

I am fed on proper meat;

You must dwell beyond the foam,

But I am safe and live at home.

Little Indian, Sioux or Crow,

Little frosty Eskimo,

Little Turk or Japanee,

Oh! don't you wish that you were me?

外国小孩

苏族或克劳族^①的印第安小孩，
满身霜雪的爱斯基摩小孩，
土耳其或日本的孩子哟，
啊！难道你们不希望是我？

你们见过红色的树林，
和大海那边的狮子群；
你们曾吃过鸵鸟蛋，
把海龟的身子掀翻。

这样的生活十分美好，
但没有我的这么美妙：
当你们四处漫步的时候，
一定常厌烦没有出国远走。

你们有奇特的食物可吃，
而我也有适合自己的肉食；
你们一定住在泛着泡沫的大海上面，
可我住在家里非常安全。

苏族或克劳族的印第安小孩，
满身霜雪的爱斯基摩小孩，
土耳其或日本的孩子哟，
啊！难道你们不希望是我？②

① 苏族和克劳族，印第安人的两个种族。
② 本诗韵律为aabb ccdd eeff gghh aabb。

083

29

The Sun's Travels

The sun is not a-bed, when I
At night upon my pillow lie;
Still round the earth his way he takes,
And morning after morning makes.

While here at home, in shining day,
We round the sunny garden play,
Each little Indian sleepy-head
Is being kissed and put to bed.

And when at eve I rise from tea,
Day dawns beyond the Atlantic Sea;
And all the children in the West
Are getting up and being dressed.

旅行的太阳

黑夜中我躺在枕上，
太阳却还没有上床；
它仍绕着地球旋转不停，
带来一个又一个黎明。

在阳光明媚的日子，
我们围着家里的花园玩个不止；
每个打瞌睡的印第安小孩，
被亲吻后放到床上来。

黄昏时我吃完茶点起身，
大西洋那边却天亮不再点灯；
西方所有的孩子们呀，
个个正在起床穿衣吧。 ①

---

① 本诗韵律为aabb ccdd eeff。

30

The Lamplighter

My tea is nearly ready and the sun has left the sky.

It's time to take the window to see Leerie going by;

For every night at teatime and before you take your seat,

With lantern and with ladder he comes posting up the street.

Now Tom would be a driver and Maria go to sea,

And my papa's a banker and as rich as he can be;

But I, when I am stronger and can choose what I'm to do,

O Leerie, I'll go round at night and light the lamps with you!

For we are very lucky, with a lamp before the door,

And Leerie stops to light it as he lights so many more;

And oh! before you hurry by with ladder and with light,

O Leerie, see a little child and nod to him to-night!

灯夫①

我的茶点快摆好时太阳已西沉，
现在又是站在窗旁看利雷走过的时辰；
每晚茶点时刻在人们坐下之前，
他就会提着灯和梯沿街出现。

瞧，汤姆要做司机，马雷亚要做水手，
爸爸在银行工作为赚钱尽力奔走；
可是我，当长大能选择工作，
利雷，我会夜晚与你一起去点灯哟！

我们很幸运，门前就有街灯一盏，
利雷停下点燃它，就像把其余的灯点燃；
啊，今夜你提着灯和梯走过的时候，
利雷呀，看看一个小孩并向他点点头。②

---

① 灯夫，指旧时点燃街灯的人。
② 本诗韵律为aabb ccdd eeff。

31

My Bed is a Boat

My bed is like a little boat;
Nurse helps me in when I embark;
She girds me in my sailor's coat
And starts me in the dark.

At night, I go on board and say
Good-night to all my friends on shore;
I shut my eyes and sail away
And see and hear no more.

And sometimes things to bed I take,

As prudent sailors have to do;

Perhaps a slice of wedding-cake,

Perhaps a toy or two.

All night across the dark we steer;

But when the day returns at last,

Safe in my room, beside the pier,

I find my vessel fast.

我的床是一只船

我的床像一只小船，
我登上船时有保姆帮忙；
她把水手服给我穿，
以便我在夜里起航。

我夜晚上船那时，
向岸上所有朋友道着晚安；
我闭上眼睛航行开始，
身边的景物和声音便全部消散。

有时我带些东西在床里放好，
谨慎的水手必须这样；
有时带的是一块结婚蛋糕，
有时把一两个玩具弄到床上。

我们整晚行驶在黑夜里，
可是当白天返回的时候，
我发现船儿的速度多么神奇——
它已安全归来停泊在码头。①

---

① 本诗韵律为abab cdcd efef ghgh。

32

The Moon

The moon has a face like the clock in the hall;

She shines on thieves on the garden wall,

On streets and fields and harbour quays,

And birdies asleep in the forks of the trees.

The squalling cat and the squeaking mouse,

The howling dog by the door of the house,

The bat that lies in bed at noon,

All love to be out by the light of the moon.

But all of the things that belong to the day

Cuddle to sleep to be out of her way;

And flowers and children close their eyes

Till up in the morning the sun shall arise.

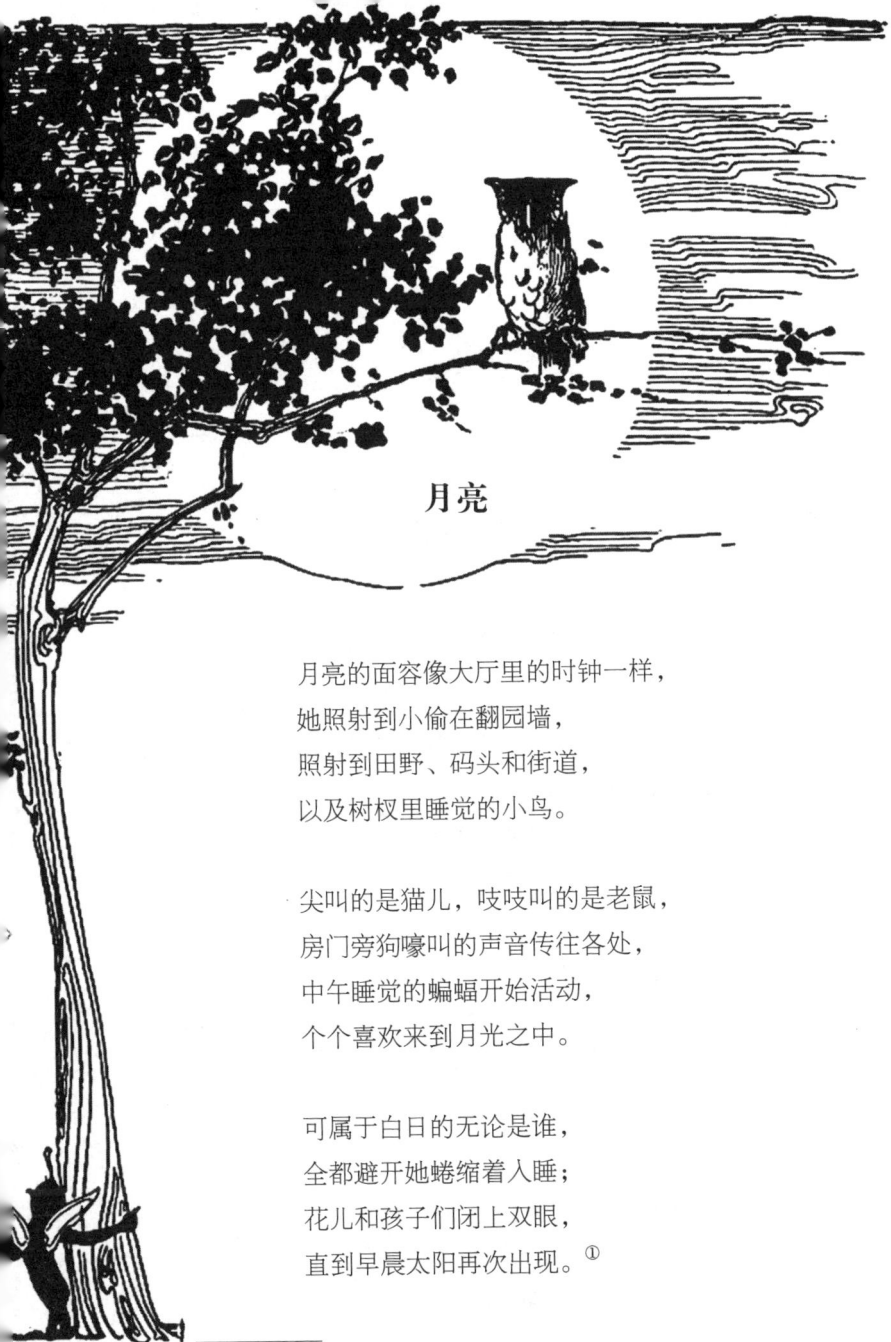

月亮

月亮的面容像大厅里的时钟一样，
她照射到小偷在翻园墙，
照射到田野、码头和街道，
以及树杈里睡觉的小鸟。

尖叫的是猫儿，吱吱叫的是老鼠，
房门旁狗嚎叫的声音传往各处，
中午睡觉的蝙蝠开始活动，
个个喜欢来到月光之中。

可属于白日的无论是谁，
全都避开她蜷缩着入睡；
花儿和孩子们闭上双眼，
直到早晨太阳再次出现。①

————————

① 本诗韵律为aabb ccdd eeff。

33

The Swing

How do you like to go up in a swing,
Up in the air so blue?
Oh, I do think it the pleasantest thing
Ever a child can do!

Up in the air and over the wall,
Till I can see so wide,
Rivers and trees and cattle and all
Over the countryside—

Till I look down on the garden green,
Down on the roof so brown—
Up in the air I go flying again,
Up in the air and down!

秋千

你对打秋千飞向空中
有什么样的感想?
啊,我认为它让孩子们共同
快乐欢喜得发狂!

升向空中飞过墙壁啦,
我看见天地多么宽广,
河流、树林、牛儿及其他,
遍布于乡村的土地之上——

然后我俯瞰花园里的绿地,
俯瞰褐色的房顶——
接着又向空中飞去,
并从空中再次向下滑行![1]

———————

[1] 本诗韵律为abab cdcd efef。

Time to Rise

A birdie with a yellow bill

Hopped upon my window sill,

Cocked his shining eye and said:

"Ain't you 'shamed, you sleepy-head!"

起床时刻

一只黄嘴小鸟

在我窗台上欢跳，

它抬起闪亮的眼睛对我唱起歌：

"你不害臊吗，这时还睡着！" ①

① 本诗韵律为aabb。

Looking-Glass River

Smooth it glides upon its travel,

Here a wimple, there a gleam—

O the clean gravel!

O the smooth stream!

Sailing blossoms, silver fishes,

Paven pools as clear as air—

How a child wishes

To live down there!

We can see our colored faces

Floating on the shaken pool

Down in cool places,

Dim and very cool;

Till a wind or water wrinkle,

Dipping marten, plumping trout,

Spreads in a twinkle

And blots all out.

See the rings pursue each other;
All below grows black as night,
Just as if mother
Had blown out the light!

Patience, children, just a minute—
See the spreading circles die;
The stream and all in it
Will clear by-and-by.

镜子河

它一直向前流去，静静地，
这儿一个涟漪那儿一个闪烁，
啊，洁净的沙砾！
啊，平静的小河！

花儿和银色的鱼在水里游荡，
它们遍布如空气般明净的深潭——
孩子多么希望
生活在里面。

我们可以看见五颜六色的面庞
漂浮在摇动的深潭里，

那是凉爽的地方，
面庞也凉爽但不清晰。

直到吹来一股风，细波不断，
有貂往水里钻，鲑往水里扑，
河水闪耀着慢慢扩散，
使一切变得模糊。

眼见水圈先后前进，
下面一切黑如夜晚，
那情景就像母亲
刚把灯灭完。

孩子们耐心等待一会儿吧——
看，扩散的水圈渐渐不在，
里面的水和所有一切呀，
很快变得清澈起来。①

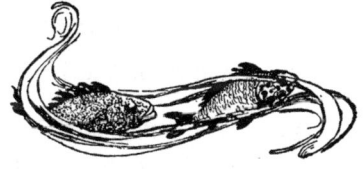

———————

① 本诗韵律为abab cdcd efef ghgh ijij klkl。

101

36

Fairy Bread

Come up here, O dusty feet!

Here is fairy bread to eat.

Here in my retiring room,

Children, you may dine

On the golden smell of broom

And the shade of pine;

And when you have eaten well,

Fairy stories hear and tell.

仙女的面包

过来吧，满脚是泥的孩子，
这儿有仙女的面包可吃。
在我休息的屋内，
孩子呀，你们可以好好分享
金雀花的美味
和松树的阴凉。
待吃饱喝足，
请把童话倾听和讲述。[①]

---

① 本诗韵律为aabcbcdd，此种韵律不多见。

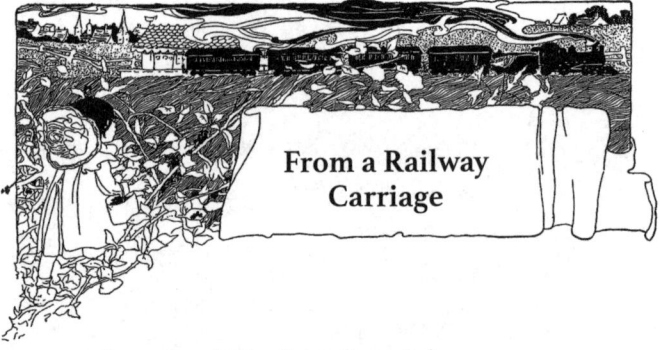

37

From a Railway Carriage

Faster than fairies, faster than witches,

Bridges and houses, hedges and ditches;

And charging along like troops in a battle

All through the meadows the horses and cattle:

All of the sights of the hill and the plain

Fly as thick as driving rain;

And ever again, in the wink of an eye,

Painted stations whistle by.

Here is a child who clambers and scrambles,

All by himself and gathering brambles;

Here is a tramp who stands and gazes;

And there is the green for stringing the daisies!

Here is a cart run away in the road

Lumping along with man and load;

And here is a mill, and there is a river:

Each a glimpse and gone for ever!

在列车车厢里

列车快过女巫，快过仙女，
眼前是桥梁和房屋，树篱和沟渠；
像战场上的军队猛冲向前，
在整个草地上马和牛随处可见：
小山和平原的这一切景物，
像瓢泼大雨猛飘到各处。
就在眨眼的片刻，
车站又呼啸而过，它们涂上彩色。
那儿有个孩子向上翻爬，
他是在独自采摘树莓吧；
那儿有个流浪汉站着凝望，
那儿的草地上雏菊成行；
那儿一辆马车在路上慢行，
拉着一个男人和东西笨重地前进；
这儿是一座磨坊，那儿是一条河川：
每个景物一闪而过，从此消失不见！①

---

① 本诗韵律为aabbccddeeffgghh。

38

Winter-Time

Late lies the wintry sun a-bed,
A frosty, fiery sleepy-head;
Blinks but an hour or two; and then,
A blood-red orange, sets again.

Before the stars have left the skies,
At morning in the dark I rise;
And shivering in my nakedness,
By the cold candle, bathe and dress.

Close by the jolly fire I sit
To warm my frozen bones a bit;
Or with a reindeer-sled, explore
The colder countries round the door.

When to go out, my nurse doth wrap
Me in my comforter and cap;
The cold wind burns my face, and blows
Its frosty pepper up my nose.

Black are my steps on silver sod;
Thick blows my frosty breath abroad;
And tree and house, and hill and lake,
Are frosted like a wedding cake.

冬天

冬天的太阳迟迟不起床，
困倦的它在严寒中散发出红光；
待眨过一两个小时眼之后，
这个血红的橘子又落下山头。

在星星离开天空以前，
早晨天没亮我就睁开了双眼；
我浑身发抖赤身裸体，
在寒冷的烛光中洗澡穿衣。

我坐下时紧靠宜人的炉火，
把冻僵的身子稍微暖和；
或者驾一辆驯鹿雪橇，
到房子周围更冷的地方嬉闹。

离开时我的保姆
让我戴上围巾和帽子才准外出；
寒风将我的脸刮得发痛，
像把结霜的胡椒粉吹入我鼻孔。

在银白色草地上我的脚印是黑色，
呼出的气立即凝固在隆冬时节；
树木与房屋，湖水与小山，
全部冻得像婚礼蛋糕一般。①

---

① 本诗韵律为aabb ccdd eeff gghh iijj。

The Hayloft

Through all the pleasant meadow-side
The grass grew shoulder-high,
Till the shining scythes went far and wide
And cut it down to dry.

Those green and sweetly smelling crops
They led the waggons home;
And they piled them here in mountain tops
For mountaineers to roam.

Here is Mount Clear, Mount Rusty-Nail,
Mount Eagle and Mount High; —
The mice that in these mountains dwell,
No happier are than I!

Oh, what a joy to clamber there,
Oh, what a place for play,
With the sweet, the dim, the dusty air,
The happy hills of hay!

干草棚

这令人惬意的广阔草地，
草长得齐肩，
直到闪亮的镰刀把它们一起
砍倒晒干。

他们用马车拉回
散发清香的庄稼，
然后把它们垒成高高的小山堆，
供登山者去翻爬。

这儿有"无云山""锈钉山"
"雄鹰山""千仞山"哟——
老鼠们就居住在中间，
却没我这般快活！

啊，在那儿爬山多么心欢，
啊，这真是一个玩耍的好地方！
这些快乐的干草山，
虽然空气中有灰尘，但也有芳香！ ①

---

① 本诗韵律为abab cdcd efef ghgh。

Farewell to the Farm

The coach is at the door at last;
The eager children, mounting fast
And kissing hands, in chorus sing:
Good-bye, good-bye, to everything!

To house and garden, field and lawn,
The meadow-gates we swang upon,
To pump and stable, tree and swing,
Good-bye, good-bye, to everything!

And fare you well for evermore,
O ladder at the hayloft door,
O hayloft where the cobwebs cling,
Good-bye, good-bye, to everything!

Crack goes the whip, and off we go;
The trees and houses smaller grow;
Last, round the woody turn we swing:
Good-bye, good-bye, to everything!

告别农场

马车终于来到门旁啦，
孩子个个急着往上爬；
吻着只只手儿，齐声歌唱：
再见，再见，所有一切——不管哪样！

告别田野和草坪，房子和花园，
我们绕过牧场的大门边；
告别树木和秋千，抽水机和马房，
再见，再见，所有一切——不管哪样！

再见，这里的各种东西，
啊，干草棚门旁的楼梯，
啊，干草棚——各处有蛛丝密布在上，
再见，再见，所有一切——不管哪样！

马鞭噼啪作响，我们越走越远，
树木和房屋渐渐变成小圆点；
终于，我们绕过树林的转弯处，歌声悠扬：
再见，再见，所有一切——不管哪样！①

---

① 本诗韵律为aabb ccbb ddbb eebb。

North-West Passage

① Good Night

When the bright lamp is carried in,
The sunless hours again begin;
O'er all without, in field and lane,
The haunted night returns again.

Now we behold the embers flee
About the firelit hearth; and see
Our faces painted as we pass,
Like pictures, on the window glass.

Must we to bed indeed? Well then,
Let us arise and go like men,
And face with an undaunted tread
The long black passage up to bed.

Farewell, O brother, sister, sire!
O pleasant party round the fire!
The songs you sing, the tales you tell,
Till far to-morrow, fare you well!

② Shadow March

All around the house is the jet-black night;

It stares through the window-pane;

It crawls in the corners, hiding from the light,

And it moves with the moving flame.

Now my little heart goes a-beating like a drum,

With the breath of the Bogies in my hair;

And all around the candle and the crooked shadows come,

And go marching along up the stair.

The shadow of the balusters, the shadow of the lamp,

The shadow of the child that goes to bed—

All the wicked shadows coming, tramp, tramp, tramp,

With the black night overhead.

③ In Port

Last, to the chamber where I lie
My fearful footsteps patter nigh,
And come out from the cold and gloom
Into my warm and cheerful room.

There, safe arrived, we turn about
To keep the coming shadows out,
And close the happy door at last
On all the perils that we past.

Then, when mamma goes by to bed,
She shall come in with tip-toe tread,
And see me lying warm and fast
And in the Land of Nod at last.

西北之旅

之一：晚安

当明亮的灯光来到屋子，
没有太阳的时候再次开始；
在田野和小巷，在整个外边，
无不重现鬼魂出没的夜晚。

我们看到炉膛里的火在燃烧，
灰烬纷纷逃跑，
我们路过时看见自己面庞
像图画般绘在窗玻璃上。

我们一定得睡觉吗？唔，
让咱们起来像大人那样迈步，
面对通向睡眠的长夜之旅，
英勇无畏地向前走去。

再见啦，兄弟、姐妹和大人，
啊，还有炉旁快乐的人们！
你们讲的故事，你们唱的歌，
到遥远的明天，再见了！①

---

① 本诗韵律为aabb ccdd eeff gghh。

之二：行进的影子

房屋四周环绕着漆黑的夜晚，
它紧紧盯住窗格之中；
它躲避灯光，在角落里爬行不断，
随着移动的光辉移动。

我小小的心儿怦怦响得像鼓，
头发里似乎有妖怪在呼吸；
影子围着烛光和弯曲的道路，
向前行进爬上了楼梯。

栏杆有影子，灯有影子，
影子还伴随上床睡觉的小孩——
一切捣蛋的影儿行进不止，
夜色在头上无处不在。①

———————
① 本诗韵律为abab cdcd efef。

之三：在港口

我终于来到寝室之中，
我不安的脚步还在附近踏动，
它们从寒冷阴暗的外边，
钻入我温暖舒适的小屋里面。

我们已安然到港，转动身子，
要让黑影在外面停止；
我们终于将快乐的门关上，
把经过的所有危险阻挡。

这时妈妈走过去睡觉，
她先走进我屋子，踮着双脚，
她会看到我周身暖洋洋，
终于躺在睡梦之乡。①

---

① 本诗韵律为aabb ccdd eedd。

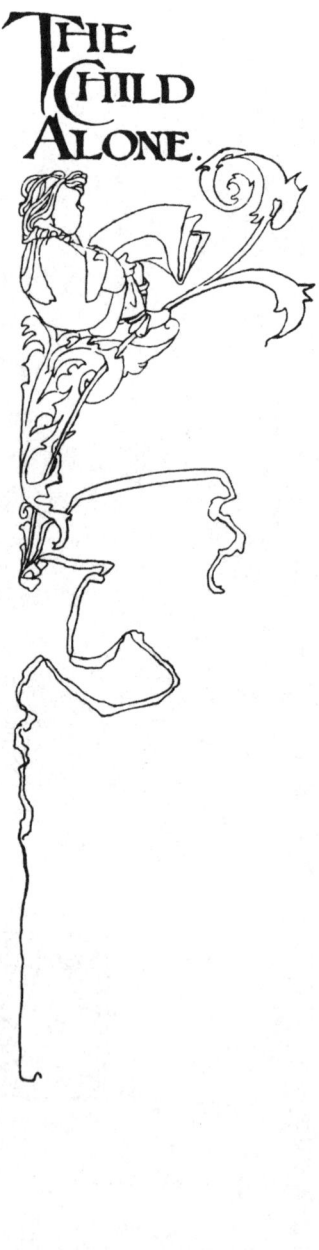

THE CHILD ALONE.

The
Child Alone

第 二 辑
孤独的孩子

The Unseen Playmate

When children are playing alone on the green,

In comes the playmate that never was seen.

When children are happy and lonely and good,

The Friend of the Children comes out of the wood.

Nobody heard him and nobody saw,

His is a picture you never could draw,

But he's sure to be present, abroad or at home,

When children are happy and playing alone.

He lies in the laurels, he runs on the grass,
He sings when you tinkle the musical glass;
Whene'er you are happy and cannot tell why,
The Friend of the Children is sure to be by!

He loves to be little, he hates to be big,
'T is he that inhabits the caves that you dig;
'T is he when you play with your soldiers of tin
That sides with the Frenchmen and never can win.

'T is he, when at night you go off to your bed,
Bids you go to sleep and not trouble your head;
For wherever they're lying, in cupboard or shelf,
'T is he will take care of your playthings himself!

隐身的游戏伙伴

当孩子们独自在草地上做游戏，
隐身的游戏伙伴就来与他们一起。
当孩子们快乐、听话但孤独，
这位孩子的朋友便会从林中走出。

既没人听见他又没人看见他，
他是一幅永远画不出的图画。
但他肯定存在，无论户内户外——
当孩子们独自做游戏，心情欢快。

他奔跑于草地，躺在月桂树上，
你用玻璃杯奏起乐曲他就把歌儿欢唱；
当你高兴但不知什么原因，
必定是这位孩子的朋友来临！

他喜欢做小孩不喜欢长大，
住在你挖的洞里的正是他呀；
当你们用锡做的士兵玩耍比赛，
正是他站在法国人一边始终被打败。

当夜晚来到你上床睡觉，
正是他祝愿你一定睡好；
你的玩具放在橱里或架上不用去管，
因为他会亲自为你细心照看！ ①

---

① 本诗韵律为aabb ccdd eeff gghh iijj，中文译诗部分韵脚有重复。

2

My Ship and I

O it's I that am the captain of a tidy little ship,
Of a ship that goes a sailing on the pond;
And my ship it keeps a-turning all around and all about;
But when I'm a little older, I shall find the secret out
How to send my vessel sailing on beyond.

For I mean to grow a little as the dolly at the helm,
And the dolly I intend to come alive;
And with him beside to help me, it's a-sailing I shall go,
It's a-sailing on the water, when the jolly breezes blow
And the vessel goes a dive-dive-dive.

O it's then you'll see me sailing through the rushes and the reeds,
And you'll hear the water singing at the prow;
For beside the dolly sailor, I'm to voyage and explore,
To land upon the island where no dolly was before,
And to fire the penny cannon in the bow.

我与船

我是一只整洁小船的船长，
船儿航行在池塘里；
一直不停地绕着圈；
当长大一些后，我将发现
让它驶向远方的秘密。

等我长大一点，像那个掌舵的洋娃娃，
我要让它像有生命一样活动；
让它在旁帮我，助我驶向前方；
我们任快活的微风吹拂，航行在水上，
船儿一次次潜入水中。

啊，你会看见我穿过灯芯草和芦苇，
你会听见水在船头唱歌谣；
因为我让洋娃娃水手陪着，航行探险去；
登上从没有过洋娃娃的岛屿，
在船头发射便宜的小炮。①

---

① 本诗韵律为abccb deffe ghiih，此种韵律不多见。

3

My Kingdom

Down by a shining water well
I found a very little dell,
No higher than my head.
The heather and the gorse about
In summer bloom were coming out,
Some yellow and some red.

I called the little pool a sea;
The little hills were big to me;
For I am very small.
I made a boat, I made a town,
I searched the caverns up and down,
And named them one and all.

And all about was mine, I said,
The little sparrows overhead,
The little minnows too.
This was the world and I was king;

For me the bees came by to sing,
For me the swallows flew.

I played there were no deeper seas,
Nor any wider plains than these,
Nor other kings than me.
At last I heard my mother call
Out from the house at evenfall,
To call me home to tea.

And I must rise and leave my dell,
And leave my dimpled water well,
And leave my heather blooms.
Alas! and as my home I neared,
How very big my nurse appeared.
How great and cool the rooms!

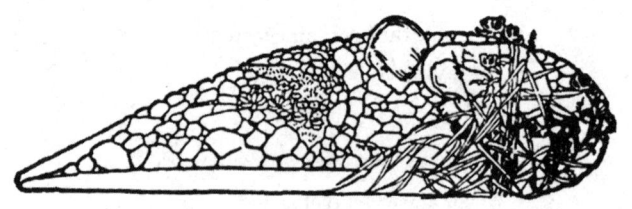

我的王国

在下面闪闪发光的水池边，
有个很小的谷被我发现，
它还没有我的头高。
周围有石楠花和荆豆花，
在夏天里竞相开放啦，
黄色和红色都可见到。

我把这小池叫作海呀，
小小的山丘对我来说很大，
因为我只是一个小小的孩子。
我建了一座镇，造了一只船，
我在山洞里来回寻探，
给所有东西起了名字。

周围一切都是我的，我说，
头上有小麻雀在飞过，
水里有小鱼在游动。
我就是这个世界的国王，
蜜蜂飞过时为我歌唱，
燕子也飞着向我这边猛冲。

没有比我游戏中更深的海洋，
也没有任何草原比它更广，
除我之外也没别的国王吧。
最后黄昏时我听见
妈妈从家里大声地喊，
叫我回去吃茶点啦。

我必须起身与小谷告别，
与泛着涟漪的水池告别，
还要与我的石楠花说再见。
哎呀！当我即将走进家门，
看到我的保姆简直是个巨人，
唉，多么庞大和冷清——那些房间！①

---

① 本诗整体韵律为aabccb ddeffe……，部分韵脚有重复，此种韵律不
多见。

Picture-Books in Winter

Summer fading, winter comes—
Frosty mornings, tingling thumbs,
Window robins, winter rooks,
And the picture story-books.

Water now is turned to stone
Nurse and I can walk upon;
Still we find the flowing brooks
In the picture story-books.

All the pretty things put by,
Wait upon the children's eye,
Sheep and shepherds, trees and crooks,
In the picture story-books.

We may see how all things are
Seas and cities, near and far,
And the flying fairies' looks,
In the picture story-books.

How am I to sing your praise,
Happy chimney-corner days,
Sitting safe in nursery nooks,
Reading picture story-books?

冬天的图画书

夏天早已过去，冬天到来——
手指变得麻木，早晨处处有霜在，
窗旁有知更鸟，天上有白嘴鸦，
我这儿有图画书啦。

水变得像石头，
我和保姆可以在上面行走；
但在这些图画里呀，
仍能看见流动的小溪啦。

一切可爱的东西呈现在眼前，
让孩子们美美地观看，
看我的图画书里呀，
这些羊与牧羊人，树与弯弯的河吧。

我们能看见所有东西的样子，
不光远近的海洋和城市，
还有天上飞行的仙女呀——
就是在这些图画里啦。

待在壁炉角里的快乐时光，
我该怎样把你们赞扬？
我们安然坐在托儿所的角落呀，
看着这些图画啦。^①

---

① 本诗韵律为aabb ccbb ddbb eebb ffbb。

5

My Treasures

These nuts, that I keep in the back of the nest,
Where all my tin soldiers are lying at rest,
Were gathered in Autumn by nursie and me
In a wood with a well by the side of the sea.

This whistle we made (and how clearly it sounds!)
By the side of a field at the end of the grounds.
Of a branch of a plane, with a knife of my own,
It was nursie who made it, and nursie alone!

The stone, with the white and the yellow and grey,
We discovered I cannot tell HOW far away;
And I carried it back although weary and cold,
For though father denies it, I'm sure it is gold.

But of all my treasures the last is the king,
For there's very few children possess such a thing;
And that is a chisel, both handle and blade,
Which a man who was really a carpenter made.

我的珍宝

我把坚果保存在巢穴里，
我所有的锡兵正躺在这儿休息；
坚果是我和保姆在秋天收集得来，
它们来自海边的林里，那儿有个水井存在。

我们做出这只口哨（它的声音多么清楚！），
在地头一个田边之处。
保姆用我的小刀，将一根梧桐树枝砍削，
独自一人把它做好！

那块宝石，带着白、黄、灰三色，
我说不出在多远把它寻得；
尽管既累又冷，可我还是将它搬回，
我肯定它是金子，虽然爸爸说这才不会。

但我的珍宝中最重要的是那个国王，
因为很少的孩子才有一种东西像这样；
那是一只有手柄的凿子，
由一个真正的木工所制。①

———————

① 本诗韵律为aabb ccdd eeff gghh。

6

Block City

What are you able to build with your blocks?
Castles and palaces, temples and docks.
Rain may keep raining, and others go roam,
But I can be happy and building at home.

Let the sofa be mountains, the carpet be sea,
There I'll establish a city for me:
A kirk and a mill and a palace beside,
And a harbour as well where my vessels may ride.

Great is the palace with pillar and wall,
A sort of a tower on the top of it all,
And steps coming down in an orderly way
To where my toy vessels lie safe in the bay.

This one is sailing and that one is moored:

Hark to the song of the sailors aboard!

And see, on the steps of my palace, the kings

Coming and going with presents and things!

Now I have done with it, down let it go!

All in a moment the town is laid low.

Block upon block lying scattered and free,

What is there left of my town by the sea?

Yet as I saw it, I see it again,

The kirk and the palace, the ships and the men,

And as long as I live and where'er I may be,

I'll always remember my town by the sea.

积木城

你能用积木把什么建好？
城堡与宫殿，码头与寺庙。
雨不停地下着， 别人在四处游荡，
但我待在家里建造城市，心情舒畅。

把沙发当山，把地毯当海，
我要在此为自己把城市建起来：
旁边有教堂、工厂和宫殿，
还有海港让我能停船。

宏伟的宫殿有高墙和大柱，
但最高的是塔楼，它最为突出，
只见梯级整整齐齐从上至下，
伸到我船儿安全停泊的海港啦。

这只船儿航行，那只船儿停泊：
你听，船上水手在唱歌哟！
瞧呀，在我宫殿的梯级之上，
国王们带着礼物你来我往！

现在，我将搭好的城市推倒，
城里的一切便消失再也找不到。
一块块积木四处散落着，
我的海边之城还剩下什么？

这过去的城市如今又浮现在眼前，
那些船儿和人们，那座教堂和宫殿，
只要我活着，无论走到哪里，
这座海边之城都会留存于我的记忆。①

---

① 本诗韵律为aabb ccdd……，部分韵脚有重复。

7

The Land of Story-Books

At evening when the lamp is lit,
Around the fire my parents sit;
They sit at home and talk and sing,
And do not play at anything.

Now, with my little gun, I crawl
All in the dark along the wall,
And follow round the forest track
Away behind the sofa back.

There, in the night, where none can spy,
All in my hunter's camp I lie,
And play at books that I have read
Till it is time to go to bed.

These are the hills, these are the woods,
These are my starry solitudes;
And there the river by whose brink
The roaring lions come to drink.

I see the others far away
As if in firelit camp they lay,
And I, like to an Indian scout,
Around their party prowled about.

So when my nurse comes in for me,
Home I return across the sea,
And go to bed with backward looks
At my dear land of Story-books.

故事书中的世界

傍晚时灯被点亮，
父母便坐在炉火一旁；
他们待在家里唱歌又谈话，
却没有任何游戏玩耍。

黑夜里我拿着小枪一支，
沿着墙壁爬行不止，
我绕过林荫小道，
从沙发背后溜掉。

黑夜里我躺在自己的猎人营地，
谁也不能发现我在哪里，
我翻动自己读过的书本，
直到该睡觉的时辰。

这儿有一些小山，那儿有一片树木，
这儿有我星光闪耀的隐秘之处，
那儿有一条河流哟，
咆哮的狮子们到河边饮水啰。

我看见远处有别人在睡觉，
好像他们在帐篷之内躺倒，
我像一个印第安侦察员，
绕着他们爬行侦探。

保姆为了找我进来，
我才回家，穿过大海，
我恋恋不舍地去睡觉——
这故事书中的世界可真好。①

---

① 本诗韵律为aabb ccdd eeff gghh iijj kkll，中文译诗中部分韵脚有
重复。

8

Armies in the Fire

The lamps now glitter down the street;

Faintly sound the falling feet;

And the blue even slowly falls

About the garden trees and walls.

Now in the falling of the gloom

The red fire paints the empty room:

And warmly on the roof it looks,

And flickers on the back of books.

Armies march by tower and spire

Of cities blazing, in the fire; —

Till as I gaze with staring eyes,

The armies fade, the lustre dies.

Then once again the glow returns;

Again the phantom city burns;

And down the red-hot valley, lo!

The phantom armies marching go!

Blinking embers, tell me true

Where are those armies marching to,

And what the burning city is

That crumbles in your furnaces!

火光中的军队

这时沿街闪烁着一盏盏灯，
同时传来轻轻的脚步声，
蓝天甚至也在慢慢落下，
落在花园的林里和墙脚啦。

夜色越来越浓，
火光把空屋染红：
它温暖地将屋顶照耀，
又把书的背面射到。

军队从高塔旁边走过，
高塔所在的城市正燃着大火——

我一直目不转睛地看着，
直到军队倒下，火光熄了。

然后红红的火光再次出现，
幻影中的城市又被点燃；
看呀！在那火红的山谷当中，
幻影里的队伍正向前行动！

闪光的灰烬请告诉我实情，
那些军队正向哪儿行进；
在你炉火中化为灰烬的城市，
都各自叫什么名字？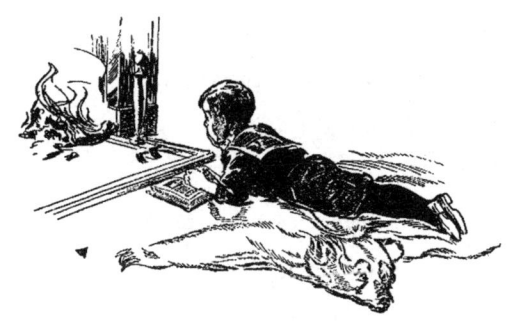

---

① 本诗韵律为aabb ccdd eeff gghh iijj kkll。

9

The Little Land

When at home alone I sit

And am very tired of it,

I have just to shut my eyes

To go sailing through the skies—

To go sailing far away

To the pleasant Land of Play;

To the fairy land afar

Where the Little People are;

Where the clover-tops are trees,

And the rain-pools are the seas,

And the leaves, like little ships

Sail about on tiny trips;

And above the Daisy tree

Through the grasses,
High o'erhead the Bumble Bee
Hums and passes.

In that forest to and fro
I can wander, I can go;
See the spider and the fly,
And the ants go marching by
Carrying parcels with their feet
Down the green and grassy street.
I can in the sorrel sit
Where the ladybird alit.
I can climb the jointed grass;
And on high
See the greater swallows pass
In the sky,
And the round sun rolling by
Heeding no such things as I.

Through that forest I can pass
Till, as in a looking-glass,
Humming fly and daisy tree
And my tiny self I see,

Painted very clear and neat
On the rain-pool at my feet.
Should a leaflet come to land
Drifting near to where I stand,
Straight I'll board that tiny boat
Round the rain-pool sea to float.

Little thoughtful creatures sit
On the grassy coasts of it;
Little things with lovely eyes
See me sailing with surprise.
Some are clad in armour green—
  (These have sure to battle been!) —
Some are pied with ev'ry hue,
Black and crimson, gold and blue;
Some have wings and swift are gone; —
But they all look kindly on.

When my eyes I once again
Open, and see all things plain:
High bare walls, great bare floor;
Great big knobs on drawer and door;

Great big people perched on chairs,

Stitching tucks and mending tears,

Each a hill that I could climb,

And talking nonsense all the time—

O dear me,

That I could be

A sailor on a the rain-pool sea,

A climber in the clover tree,

And just come back, a sleepy-head,

Late at night to go to bed.

小小的地方

当独自坐在家里玩，
我便感到非常厌烦，
于是把眼睛紧紧闭拢，
想象着航行穿过天空——
我航行到很远的地方，
到快乐的"游戏世界"之上，
到遥远的仙境地带；
那儿有"小人"存在，
那儿三叶草成了树子，
海洋不过是雨池；
片片叶儿像小船，
在小小的旅程中打转；
大黄蜂嗡嗡地叫，
在雏菊上空回响，
又穿过了绿草，
高高地在我头上回荡。

我可以在那片森林，
来来回回漫行，
看苍蝇和蜘蛛
还有蚂蚁向前迈步，
它们用脚拖着东西一包包，
前进，沿着绿荫小道，
我可以坐在酢浆草里，
瓢虫也飞落到此地。
我可以爬上有节头的草茎，
于高处
看大燕在天上飞行，
翩翩起舞。
圆圆的太阳在天空旋转，
我注意的东西它根本没看见。

我可以穿过森林，
直到好像看见雏菊、嗡嗡叫的苍蝇
和渺小的我自己，
被描绘在脚旁的雨池里，
那图像多么清楚整洁，
像在镜中一般，真的。
假如有一片小叶靠岸，
漂到我站的岸边，
我会直接登上这小船往前走，
绕着大海般的雨池漂流。

富有思想的动物只只都很小，
它们坐在岸边，这儿草叶繁茂；
小小生命长着可爱的眼睛，
看见我航行十分震惊。
有的身穿绿色铠甲——
（它们一定上过战场啦！）；
有的身上有各种色彩，
黑、红、金、蓝样样俱在；
有的长着翅膀很快飞离——
但它们看起来无不带着善意。

当我再次把眼睛睁开，
一切东西看得明白：
空旷的地板，光秃的高墙；

大大的球形把手在抽屉与门上；
高大的人们坐在椅子里，
缝着褶皱，补着破衣；
他们是一座座山我可以往上爬，
自始至终说着废话——
哎呀呀，
看我能做啥吧——
我能在像大海的雨池里航行，
在树一样的三叶草上攀行，
回家时我相当困倦，
因为已是早该睡觉的夜晚。①

---

① 本诗韵律大多为aabbccddeeffgghhiijj，个别地方有点变化。诗中部
分韵脚有重复。

GARDEN DAYS.

Garden Days

第 三 辑
花园里的日子

1

Night and Day

When the golden day is done,

Through the closing portal,

Child and garden, Flower and sun,

Vanish all things mortal.

As the blinding shadows fall

As the rays diminish,

Under evening's cloak, they all

Roll away and vanish.

Garden darkened, daisy shut,
Child in bed, they slumber—
Glow-worm in the hallway rut,
Mice among the lumber.

In the darkness houses shine,
Parents move the candles;
Till on all, the night divine
Turns the bedroom handles.

Till at last the day begins
In the east a-breaking,
In the hedges and the whins
Sleeping birds a-waking.

In the darkness shapes of things,
Houses, trees and hedges,
Clearer grow; and sparrow's wings
Beat on window ledges.

These shall wake the yawning maid;
She the door shall open—
Finding dew on garden glade
And the morning broken.

There my garden grows again

Green and rosy painted,

As at eve behind the pane

From my eyes it fainted.

Just as it was shut away,

Toy-like, in the even,

Here I see it glow with day

Under glowing heaven.

Every path and every plot,

Every blush of roses,

Every blue forget-me-not

Where the dew reposes,

"Up!" they cry, "the day is come

On the smiling valleys:

We have beat the morning drum;

Playmate, join your allies!"

昼夜

当金色的一天
从关闭的大门消失，
花儿与太阳，孩子与花园，
一切生物把活动停止。

当炫目的影子落下，
当太阳的光线减退，
一切便被夜色笼罩啦，
它们无不纷纷退回。

雏菊合拢，花园变暗，
孩子上床睡觉已安静——
萤火虫闪烁在走廊里面，
老鼠在杂物间穿行。

房子在黑夜里发出亮光，
父母们端着蜡烛忙碌；
直到卧室的门拉手转向
外面神圣的黑暗之处。

直到次日天光微亮，
东方泛起了鱼肚白，
在树篱和荆豆上，
睡觉的鸟儿刚刚醒来。

各种东西的形状——
房子、树木和树篱呀，
这时变得越来越明朗，
麻雀的翅膀把窗台拍打。

女仆醒来时会打着呵欠，
然后她去打开房门——
花园道上的露珠被她发现，
知道这是又一个早晨。

我的花园再次涂有
红和绿的颜色，
就像黄昏时我站在窗后
看见它们慢慢消失了。

我的花园在黄昏时呀，
像玩具一样被收回，
我这时见它在晴朗的天空下，
与白日一道熠熠生辉。

每一块地每一条道，
每一束红润的玫瑰，
每一根蓝色的勿忘草，
都有露珠仍在安睡。

"快起来！"它们叫着，
"白天来到了微笑的山谷：
我们已把晨鼓敲响哟；
伙伴们，快快来加入！"①

---

① 本诗韵律为abab cdcd efef ghgh……，中文译诗中部分韵脚有重复。

2

Nest Eggs

Birds all the sunny day
Flutter and quarrel
Here in the arbour-like
Tent of the laurel.

Here in the fork
The brown nest is seated;
Four little blue eggs
The mother keeps heated.

While we stand watching her
Staring like gabies,
Safe in each egg are the
Bird's little babies.

Soon the frail eggs they shall
Chip, and upspringing
Make all the April woods
Merry with singing.

Younger than we are,

O children, and frailer,

Soon in the blue air they'll be,

Singer and sailor.

We, so much older,

Taller and stronger,

We shall look down on the

Birdies no longer.

They shall go flying

With musical speeches

High overhead in the

Tops of the beeches.

In spite of our wisdom

And sensible talking,

We on our feet must go

Plodding and walking.

巢中的蛋

晴天里鸟儿们整天
吵闹和飞动
在这凉亭般的
月桂树冠中。

褐色的鸟巢筑在
这树杈里面；
鸟妈妈一直孵着
四只蓝色的小蛋。

我们站着看它
呆呆地注视，
每一只鸟宝宝
都安全藏在每个蛋里。

不久它们把蛋壳啄破，
从中腾飞起来，
让整个四月的林中
欢乐的歌声无处不在。

啊，孩子们，
它们比我们更弱更小，
可不久就能在蓝天里
飞行和欢叫。

我们远比它们更大，
也更壮和更高，
可是却再也不能
俯瞰那些小鸟。

它们振翅高飞，
说着悦耳的语言——
翱翔于我们头上，
翱翔于山毛榉顶端。

虽然我们有智慧，
能明智地把话谈，
但我们必须步行，
沉重又缓慢。①

---

① 本诗总体韵律为abcb defe ghih......，有少量重复韵脚。

3

The Flowers

All the names I know from nurse:
Gardener's garters, Shepherd's purse,
Bachelor's buttons, Lady's smock,
And the Lady Hollyhock.

Fairy places, fairy things,
Fairy woods where the wild bee wings,
Tiny trees for tiny dames—
These must all be fairy names!

Tiny woods below whose boughs
Shady fairies weave a house;
Tiny tree-tops, rose or thyme,
Where the braver fairies climb!

Fair are grown-up people's trees,
But the fairest woods are these;
Where, if I were not so tall,
I should live for good and all.

花儿

花儿们的名字我从保姆那里知道：
纽扣花，酢浆草，
花叶草芦，荠菜，
还有女士葵处处存在。

仙境般的地方，仙子们的东西，
野蜂飞行在仙境般的树林里，
小小树儿为小小少女生长呀——
它们一定都有仙子般的名字吧！

在小小林子的树枝下面，
仙子们暗自把房屋搭建；
勇敢的仙子慢慢爬上
小小树顶——那里有玫瑰或百里香！

大人种植的树十分美丽，
但却无法与这树林相比；
如果我不是长得很高哟，
我会永远在这里生活。①

---

① 本诗韵律为aabb ccdd eeff gghh，中文译诗中部分韵脚有重复。

4

Summer Sun

Great is the sun, and wide he goes

Through empty heaven without repose

And in the blue and glowing days

More thick than rain he showers his rays.

Though closer still the blinds we pull

To keep the shady parlour cool,

Yet he will find a chink or two

To slip his golden fingers through.

The dusty attic spider-clad
He, through the keyhole, maketh glad;
And through the broken edge of tiles
Into the laddered hay-loft smiles.

Meantime his golden face around
He bares to all the garden ground,
And sheds a warm and glittering look
Among the ivy's inmost nook.

Above the hills, along the blue,
Round the bright air with footing true,
To please the child, to paint the rose,
The gardener of the World, he goes.

夏天的太阳

太阳多伟大，走得真宽广，
它不停地穿过辽阔的天上，
在天气晴朗阳光灿烂的日子里，
雨丝也不如它投下的光线稠密。

虽然它越近我们把窗帘拉得越紧，
以便让阴凉留在客厅，
但它总会找到一两个裂口，
把自己的金手指伸到里头。

积满灰尘的阁楼里蛛网密布，
它穿过锁眼照亮屋内各处；
又穿过破碎的瓦片边，
微笑着进入架着梯子的干草棚里面。

同时它转动金色的面孔
向花园里的每一个角落露出笑容，
又将它温暖闪耀的光芒
照射在常春藤最隐秘的地方。

它是世界园丁，
迈出的脚步十分坚定，
它行进在山顶上，沿着天空和大海，
装饰玫瑰又逗乐了小孩。①

---

① 本诗韵律为aabb ccdd……，部分韵脚有重复。

The Dumb Soldier

When the grass was closely mown,

Walking on the lawn alone,

In the turf a hole I found,

And hid a soldier underground.

Spring and daisies came apace;

Grasses hid my hiding place;

Grasses run like a green sea

O'er the lawn up to my knee.

Under grass alone he lies,
Looking up with leaden eyes,
Scarlet coat and pointed gun,
To the stars and to the sun.

When the grass is ripe like grain,
When the scythe is stoned again,
When the lawn is shaven clear,
Then my hole shall reappear.

I shall find him, never fear,
I shall find my grenadier;
But for all that's gone and come,
I shall find my soldier dumb.

He has lived, a little thing,
In the grassy woods of spring;
Done, if he could tell me true,
Just as I should like to do.

He has seen the starry hours
And the springing of the flowers;
And the fairy things that pass
In the forests of the grass.

In the silence he has heard
Talking bee and ladybird,
And the butterfly has flown
O'er him as he lay alone.

Not a word will he disclose,
Not a word of all he knows.
I must lay him on the shelf,
And make up the tale myself

无声的士兵

当草儿被全部割下，
我一人走在这草地上呀，
在土里发现一个洞，
我便将一个士兵藏在其中。

春天和雏菊迅速来临，
草儿把我的洞穴藏隐；
它们就像一片碧绿的海，
高度长到我的膝盖。

他独自躺在草儿下面，
两眼铅灰，制服深红，枪杆尖尖，
他抬头仰望
星星和太阳。

当草儿成熟如谷粒，
当镰刀再次被磨利，
当草地被彻底修整好，
我那个洞呀又可见到。

我会找到他的，不用怕，
我一定会找到我的步兵啦；
尽管一切事物来了又走，
但我总会找到自己的无声士兵朋友。

这个小家伙，已经生活
在春天草叶茂盛的林里啰；
如果他能告诉我实话就好了，
那些事情一定也是我想做的。

他曾见过灿烂的星光，
以及花儿不断绽放；
也见过长满草叶的林里，
路过的精灵十分神奇。

他曾默默地听见
蜜蜂和瓢虫把话谈，
当他独自躺在那儿时，
蝴蝶在他上面飞舞不止。

他一个字也不愿透露，
他知道一切却只字不吐。
我必须将他放在架上，
自己把故事编造妥当。①

---

① 本诗韵律为aabb ccdd eeff……，部分韵脚有重复。

6

Autumn Fires

In the other gardens

And all up the vale,

From the autumn bonfires

See the smoke trail!

Pleasant summer over

And all the summer flowers,

The red fire blazes,

The grey smoke towers.

Sing a song of seasons!

Something bright in all!

Flowers in the summer,

Fires in the fall!

秋火

在别家花园里，
在整个山谷间，
那秋天的篝火，
烟雾四处蔓延！

快乐的夏季过去，
带走了夏天的花，
红红的火光在照耀，
灰色的烟雾聚成高塔。

唱一支四季之歌！
每一季都十分欢快！
夏天有花朵开放，
秋天的火焰无处不在！①

① 本诗韵律为abcb defe ghih。

7

The Gardener

The gardener does not love to talk.

He makes me keep the gravel walk;

And when he puts his tools away,

He locks the door and takes the key.

Away behind the currant row,

Where no one else but cook may go,

Far in the plots, I see him dig,

Old and serious, brown and big.

He digs the flowers, green, red, and blue,

Nor wishes to be spoken to.

He digs the flowers and cuts the hay,
And never seems to want to play.

Silly gardener! summer goes,
And winter comes with pinching toes,
When in the garden bare and brown
You must lay your barrow down.

Well now, and while the summer stays,
To profit by these garden days
O how much wiser you would be
To play at Indian wars with me!

花匠

花匠不喜欢说话，
只让我把砾石路保护呀；
他将工具存放以后，
就锁好门把钥匙带走。

在那排黑醋栗后面，
只有厨子才会走到那边；
我见他在远处的地里挖着土，
年老而认真，黝黑又魁梧。

他把绿、红、蓝的花栽培上，
不想别人对他把话儿讲。

他栽培花又割掉杂草，
好像从不想把游戏玩好。

傻傻的花匠！当夏天离开，
冬天踮着脚走来，
在光秃黯淡的花园里，
你必须把手推车搁在地。

瞧呀，趁现在还是夏天，
赶快好好享受这个花园，
假如你和我玩印第安人的战斗，
啊，你将变得多么聪明和优秀！①

---

① 本诗韵律为aabb ccdd eeff gghh iijj。中文译诗中部分韵脚有重复。

Historical Associations

Dear Uncle Jim, this garden ground
That now you smoke your pipe around,
Has seen immortal actions done
And valiant battles lost and won.

Here we had best on tip-toe tread,
While I for safety march ahead,
For this is that enchanted ground
Where all who loiter slumber sound.

Here is the sea, here is the sand,
Here is the simple Shepherd's Land,
Here are the fairy hollyhocks,
And there are Ali Baba's rocks.

But yonder, see! apart and high,
Frozen Siberia lies; where I,
With Robert Bruce and William Tell,
Was bound by an enchanter's spell.

历史的联想

亲爱的叔父吉姆，在这个花园
你抽着烟斗漫步于我眼前；
你目睹了许多有输有赢的英勇战斗，
你见证过的那些壮举都将不朽。

在这儿我们最好踮着脚迈步，
为了安全，让我在前面带路，
因为这是充满魔力的地方，
所有闯入者无不发出睡眠的声响。

这儿是大海，这儿是沙滩，
这儿是简朴牧羊人的地盘；
这儿有仙境里的蜀葵，
还有阿里巴巴的岩石堆。

瞧呀！在那边远方的高地，
冰封的西伯利亚就在那里，
我与罗伯特·布鲁斯①还有威廉·退尔②一道，
被一个巫士的符咒迷倒。③

----

① 罗伯特·布鲁斯，曾经领导苏格兰王国击退英格兰王国的入侵，取得
民族独立。
② 威廉·退尔，瑞士传说中反奥地利统治、争取瑞士独立的民族英雄。
③ 本诗韵律为aabb ccdd eeff gghh。

ENVOYS.

Envoys

第 ④ 辑
结尾的诗

1

To Willie and Henrietta

If two may read aright
These rhymes of old delight
And house and garden play,
You too, my cousins, and you only, may.

You in a garden green
With me were king and queen,
Were hunter, soldier, tar,
And all the thousand things that children are.

Now in the elders' seat
We rest with quiet feet,
And from the window-bay
We watch the children, our successors, play.

"Time was," the golden head
Irrevocably said;
But time which none can bind,
While flowing fast away, leaves love behind.

献给威利和亨莉埃塔

如果有两人能读得正确
这些关于往日的喜悦，
和房子与花园里游戏的诗歌，
那么只有你们，我的表妹和表哥。

你们曾在绿色的花园里，
和我玩扮国王和王后的游戏，
你们又是猎人、士兵和水手，
孩子们扮演的成千角色样样都有。

现在我们安然地
坐在父辈的椅里，
快从窗格柱中看吧
看孩子们——我们的后代——玩耍。

"那已是过去。"杰出的人
坚定地这样赞成；
虽然没人能将时光挽留，
但它飞速流逝时已将爱留在身后。①

---

① 本诗韵律为aabb ccdd……，部分韵脚有重复。

2

To My Mother

You too, my mother, read my rhymes
For love of unforgotten times,
And you may chance to hear once more
The little feet along the floor.

献给母亲

母亲呀，为了那难忘的日子，
也请你读读我写的这些诗，
你或许会偶然再次听见
那小小的脚步声踏在地板。①

---

① 本诗韵律为aabb。

To Auntie

"Chief of our aunts"—not only I,

But all your dozen of nurselings cry—

"What did the other children do?

And what were childhood, wanting you?"

献给阿姨

"你是我们最亲爱的阿姨，"不仅我，
所有你带的孩子都这么说——
"别的那些孩子都做什么？
没有你，我们的童年又会是怎样的呢？"①

---

① 本诗韵律为aabb。

4

To Minnie

The red room with the giant bed

Where none but elders laid their head;

The little room where you and I

Did for awhile together lie

And, simple suitor, I your hand

In decent marriage did demand;

The great day nursery, best of all,

With pictures pasted on the wall

And leaves upon the blind—

A pleasant room wherein to wake

And hear the leafy garden shake

And rustle in the wind—

And pleasant there to lie in bed

And see the pictures overhead—

The wars about Sebastopol,

The grinning guns along the wall,

The daring escalade,

The plunging ships, the bleating sheep,

The happy children ankle-deep

And laughing as they wade:

All these are vanished clean away,

And the old manse is changed to-day;

It wears an altered face

And shields a stranger race.

The river, on from mill to mill,

Flows past our childhood's garden still;

But ah! we children never more

Shall watch it from the water-door!

Below the yew—it still is there—

Our phantom voices haunt the air

As we were still at play,

And I can hear them call and say:

"How far is it to Babylon?"

Ah, far enough, my dear,

Far, far enough from here—

Yet you have farther gone!

"Can I get there by candlelight?"

So goes the old refrain.

I do not know--perchance you might—

But only, children, hear it right,

Ah, never to return again!

The eternal dawn, beyond a doubt,

Shall break on hill and plain,

And put all stars and candles out

Ere we be young again.

To you in distant India, these

I send across the seas,

Nor count it far across.

For which of us forgets

The Indian cabinets,

The bones of antelope, the wings of albatross,

The pied and painted birds and beans,

The junks and bangles, beads and screens,

The gods and sacred bells,

And the load-humming, twisted shells!

The level of the parlour floor

Was honest, homely, Scottish shore;

But when we climbed upon a chair,

Behold the gorgeous East was there!

Be this a fable; and behold

Me in the parlour as of old,

And Minnie just above me set

In the quaint Indian cabinet!

Smiling and kind, you grace a shelf

Too high for me to reach myself.

Reach down a hand, my dear, and take

These rhymes for old acquaintance' sake!

献给明妮

大床放在红屋里面，
只有大人睡在里边；
在那间小屋里
我和你躺在一起，
我曾天真地牵着你的手，
郑重地向你把婚求；
那是最好的日间托儿所，
墙上贴着一张张画哟，
树叶飘落到窗帘——
这是一间快乐的屋子，

我们醒来时听见茂盛的花园摇动不止，
风中的沙沙声响个不断——
躺在床上真是快乐呀，
可以仰望着一幅幅绘画——
有关于塞瓦斯托波尔的大战，
有沿城墙放着龇牙咧嘴的枪杆，
有勇士沿云梯爬上城墙，
有将沉的轮船和咩咩叫的绵羊，
有快乐的小孩也在画上，
他们欢笑着涉水前行。
如今这一切都已彻底不见，
那古老的牧师住宅也改变，
它的模样和以前不同，
里面是些更陌生的面孔。
河水仍从一个个磨坊流过，
也从我们童年的花园流过，
但是哎呀！我们再也不能像孩子
观看它从水闸流逝！
紫杉树依旧在那里没有倒，
我们幻觉中的声音在空中萦绕，
好像我们仍然在玩游戏，
我能听见声音在叫着说：
"到巴比伦有多远哟？"

啊，亲爱的，你离这个地点，
离得遥远又遥远——
可是你却走得更加遥远！
"黄昏我是否能到那里？"
古老的副歌这样唱哩。
不知道——也许你会吧——
但是孩子们，你们听好了，
这一去，便再也不会回来！
因为，那永恒的黎明
将在山上和平原显露身影，
让所有星星和蜡烛熄完——
在我们又变得年轻以前。

我把这些诗送过大海那面，
送到在遥远印度的你身边，
别去计算我们之间的距离——
为的是不让有谁忘记：
印度人的贮柜，信天翁的翅膀，
没有斑驳的鸟儿和豆子也不应当，
还有神像与神铃，
舢板与手镯，珠子与银屏，
羚羊的骨骼，
以及嗡嗡响的螺旋贝壳！
客厅的地板

普普通通，像苏格兰的海岸；
但当我们爬到椅上，
就看见那边灿烂的东方！
这也许是一个神话，
请注意我依旧在客厅里呀，
而明妮端坐在我的上端，
就在那古雅的印度贮柜里面！
你和蔼的微笑在架子上闪耀，
可那儿太高我够不到。
亲爱的，请伸下一只手，
接受我这个老朋友的问候！①

---

① 本诗总体韵律为aabbccddeeffgghh……，部分韵脚有重复。

5

To My Name-Child

①

Some day soon this rhyming volume, if you learn with proper speed,
Little Louis Sanchez, will be given you to read.
Then you shall discover, that your name was printed down
By the English printers, long before, in London town.

In the great and busy city where the East and West are met,
All the little letters did the English printer set;
While you thought of nothing, and were still too young to play,
Foreign people thought of you in places far away.

Ay, and while you slept, a baby, over all the English lands
Other little children took the volume in their hands;
Other children questioned, in their homes across the seas:
Who was little Louis, won't you tell us, mother, please?

Now that you have spelt your lesson, lay it down and go and play,

Seeking shells and seaweed on the sands of Monterey,

Watching all the mighty whalebones, lying buried by the breeze,

Tiny sandpipers, and the huge Pacific seas.

And remember in your playing, as the sea-fog rolls to you,

Long ere you could read it, how I told you what to do;

And that while you thought of no one, nearly half the world away

Some one thought of Louis on the beach of Monterey!

献给与我同名的孩子

之一

如果你学习进度适当，那么不久的一天，
小路易斯·桑切斯呀，这本诗集就会给你看看。
那时你会发觉，在很久以前的伦敦，
你的名字已被英国印刷商印上书本。

这座东西方交汇的大都市十分繁忙，
英国印刷商任何小小的文字都能印上；
当你年幼时，什么都不想还不会做游戏，
外国人却在遥远的地方想到了你。

宝贝呀，当你在英国的土地上睡觉，
别的孩子正把这本诗集在手里捧好；
他们提着问，在大海那边自己的家：
谁是小路易斯，告诉我好吗，妈妈？①

---

① 本诗韵律为aabb ccdd eeff gghh。

之二

既然你已上完了拼写课，那么快放下书本去玩乐，
在蒙特里沙滩上寻找海草和贝壳，
看那些巨大的鲸骨，被微风埋葬，
看小小的矶鹞和辽阔的太平洋。

玩耍时海雾向你卷来，你一定要牢记，
我曾告诉你该怎样做，尽管你还不会读这些诗；
你虽然谁也没想到，但在近半个地球以外，
有人却想到这蒙特里沙滩有个路易斯在！[①]

---

① 本诗韵律为aabb ccdd。

215

6

To Any Reader

As from the house your mother sees

You playing round the garden trees,

So you may see, if you will look

Through the windows of this book,

Another child, far, far away,

And in another garden, play.

But do not think you can at all,

By knocking on the window, call

That child to hear you. He intent

Is all on his play-business bent.

He does not hear, he will not look,

Nor yet be lured out of this book.

For, long ago, the truth to say,

He has grown up and gone away,

And it is but a child of air

That lingers in the garden there.

献给所有读者

正像你母亲从屋里
看你绕着花园的树做游戏，
只要你愿意看看，
也能从这"书窗"里看见
远处有另一个孩子呀，
也在另一个花园玩耍。
但别以为你敲敲这扇书窗，
就能让那孩子听到声响。
他把整个心思一同
放在了游戏当中。
他听不到也看不到，
他不会受诱惑丢下书跑。
因为确实在很早以前，
他已长大远离不见，
剩下一个缥缈的小孩，
仍在那花园里逗留徘徊。①

---

① 本诗韵律为aabbccdd……，部分韵脚有重复。

End

完